Jonah and the Bony-Finned Asteroid Fish

Bible Society
Stonehill Green
Westlea
Swindon SN5 7DG
biblesociety.org.uk

First published 2019 by The British and Foreign Bible Society.
ISBN: 978-0-564-04737-6

good NEWS BIBLE

Design and production by Bible Society Resources Ltd, a wholly owned subsidiary of The British and Foreign Bible Society.

BSRL/1M/2019
Printed in Great Britain

JONAH

AND THE

BONY-FINNED ASTEROID FISH

JO SHERINGHAM

For the gifts and the calling of God are irrevocable.
Romans 11.29 (NRSV)

*Where can I go from your spirit?
Or where can I flee from your presence?
If I ascend to heaven, you are there;
if I make my bed in Sheol, you are there.
If I take the wings of the morning
and settle at the farthest limits of the sea,
even there your hand shall lead me,
and your right hand shall hold me fast.
If I say, 'Surely the darkness shall cover me,
and the light around me become night',
even the darkness is not dark to you;
the night is as bright as the day,
for darkness is as light to you.*
Psalm 139.7–12 (NRSV)

Contents

Part One

From Within

This is it, then. The finale. The end. Curtains. My paltry little life spat out into the oblivion of timeless space. Probably most deservedly so, I suppose.

Ah, now here's the small catch, I think. Let's see if this does the trick and maybe I will still be able to slide open the viewing plate.

I know we've hit something or landed somewhere, which was the last thing I thought was going to happen when I was stuffed into this ejection capsule. But it all happened so fast, and pondering on the whys and wherefores of such a step was not exactly paramount at the time.

There, that's got it. Now I can at least see what has, only temporarily I suspect, halted my demise.

Interesting … or, rather, quite disgusting. This is definitely organic and definitely alive!

What in all the planetary systems is this sort of black, grey slime? Just look at the size of those veins, or whatever anatomical feature they might possibly be. If I'm not mistaken, they seem to be suckering up against the side of the capsule, pulsating, oscillating … digesting …

We've been eaten. I don't believe it. That just about takes the biscuit. Me and my soon-to-be-digested, disintegrated capsule, we are the veritable biscuit!

I ask you: ejected into nothingness, into the vast expanse of space, and all along there was something in the nothingness and it's just had us for lunch.

Yes, thank you very much, my little small voice; look what happens when you try to run away.

Oh my word … we're moving! This suddenly seems rather serious and suddenly rather gruesome and I don't think it's going to be a comfortably silent, swift end, either. This is a truly horrific predicament. By the looks of those rippling membranes, we seem to be sliding further down into whatever it is that has eaten us.

I'm talking to myself, I know I'm talking to myself, I know I'm saying 'we' when it really is just 'me', but for what I presume are to be these last few minutes of my life, this capsule has suddenly become my best and dearest friend.

Jonah Son of Amittai

He was attempting to calm his thoughts and clear away any further distractions, so that he could finish his morning meditations without any more interruptions, when the bell outside his front door rang, again. Even the deep, mellow clanging of this specially chosen bell (especially chosen for its deep, mellow clanginess) did not manage to crack the finely honed porcelain exterior of the prophet, although it was not far off. With a restrained huffiness, he clambered up from his kneeling position, grunting and muttering under his breath as he gathered up his robes and waddled across the room to answer the door.

Waddling was indeed the best word for describing his gait, especially after he'd already had to get up from the floor four times in a row that morning. First, there had been a screeching disturbance from his neighbour's Mammouthian Scarry Rat named Bongadin. Second, a consignment of fresh feed for the aforementioned Bongadin had been delivered to the wrong door – his door. Third, a query from the most anxious next-door neighbour as to the whereabouts of said Bongadin – had he seen the Rat at all since last night? And fourth, the meat vendor's red-faced wife had waved a business-class cleaver in his face, asking if he was the owner of the Mammouthian Scarry Rat last witnessed escaping from their meat transporter with a side of steak! At such an early hour in the morning (it wasn't even 10 o'clock yet) and at his time of life, it was just all too much.

On reaching his front door he cracked open the viewing plate, rather sharply, to the right, to see who this fifth caller was. Perhaps this time it would actually be Bongadin the Mammouthian Scarry Rat himself, seeking asylum in the gracious bosom of a gentle prophet.

Thankfully not; it was just a message-bot, a much more everyday, expected and innocuous caller.

'Post for Jonah son of Amittai,' the voice of the message-bot crackled.

'Yes, yes, that's me.' The prophet tried not to sound too exasperated. 'I'm not opening this door again. Just plug it into the viewing plate and I'll see what it is.'

The message-bot held up the flat rectangular screen that displayed the post and clicked it into place over the viewing plate in the door; after a few seconds the screen flickered into life and the message was visible.

The prophet shuddered, not exactly with rage or fear or pain or anticipation but with all of them and something more besides. He felt pure emotion deep in the dark caverns of his soul and it was not at all comfortable.

'Will the post be accepted or wiped, sir?' questioned the message-bot.

With a strangled spitting of words, the prophet answered, 'Wiped!' and, just to make his point, he slid the viewing plate shut with as much force as he could muster.

The bell rang again. He shut his eyes, took a breath and remembered his manners; he was a prophet after all and he had standards. It was required by law to pay for any wiping of any post one might receive, and he did not want any penalties showing on his Citizen's Account. It was getting harder and harder to keep a clean slate these days.

In a more business-like manner he slid open the viewing plate once more, apologised to the message-bot who was still waiting outside (Jonah knew it was not necessary to apologise to a roving piece of service technology but it just seemed like the right thing to do) and then held his thumb-print up to the screen to register his due payment.

'Thank you, Jonah son of Amittai, have a nice day.'

'Thank you,' muttered Jonah in return.

The message-bot put his screen back inside his well-worn postbag, which looked rather fitting slung across his rusty bodywork, and turned towards his next delivery destination. Perhaps, thought Jonah, there was some post for the Mammouthian Scarry Rat.

The prophet turned around and leant his back against the door. He shut his eyes and, with a distinct firmness, placed his head back, several times, against the door. He could not be said to be exactly hitting his head against the door, but he was, almost. A great sigh found its way out between his clenched teeth; he just did not understand.

'There is no rhyme or reason behind this. It just won't do. Not at all.' He sounded muddled and desperate.

He realised he was talking to himself again. There had been a lot of that recently; however, he was rapidly coming to the conclusion that he himself was the only one worth talking to.

'This is madness. I need to get away, I need a holiday. When was the last time I had a holiday, eh? You tell me that.'

The prophet opened his eyes and stood up straight, away from the door. A gleam of resolution lifted his mature features, his spiky eyebrows standing to attention.

There was no time for meditation now. In fact, Jonah realised that that was the last thing he should do, because if he prayed, really prayed, he would be opening himself up to all sorts of trouble and the messages may never stop! He needed to make his move and escape.

No; he had caught himself out. He would not use the word 'escape', because that was not what it was. He was simply giving himself a well-earned – oh yes indeed – a very well-earned break, a rest, a bit of space, a bit of time to himself, no interruptions, no demands, no more messages.

'It can only do me good and I know this is just what I need. If the thing, the thing that I am being asked to do, is really that important, then I'm afraid I am just not the man for the job. Not today at any rate.'

The subject had been thoroughly discussed (with himself) and the decision made. Jonah son of Amittai went off to pack a bag.

The trouble was that Jonah son of Amittai was, as we have already discovered, a prophet. He was a prophet of God and, until now, a fairly decent one. There had been moments when it could be truly said he had had his moment – a moment in history when his name had been known and the words he had said had been monumental and extraordinary and pivotal. There had been a time when he'd had the ear of King Jeroboam no less, and had spoken promises from the Lord concerning the recovery of lost territories. Sometimes his name still cropped up in the odd history lesson, in the odd school, every now and then. In these latter years, though, things had all gone a bit quiet. He was still a prophet – one never stopped being a prophet, like one could never stop, he supposed, being a Mammouthian Scarry Rat who escaped with stolen meaty goods, although he thought to make a comparison with such a creature was not quite the done thing, of course.

Jonah son of Amittai was, from all that was visible to the naked eye, a prophet through and through; but after all these years the propheting was of such a habitual nature, such a routine garb, that it now covered and had almost smothered the very essence, the very connection that had brought about its being in the first place. There were deep, dark cellars in Jonah's soul, as well as in his house, where the dust grew thickly layered, covering all the naïve newness of those earlier, simpler years. However, all was not lost, and it never would be while he still claimed the title of prophet: he had received a call, or rather several posts, from a steady run of message-bots over recent weeks, all with the same message. God had a job for him, and (although Jonah did not think for one second it was true and neither did he want it to be true) he was, it seemed, just the man.

'Ridiculous, a ridiculous idea! It just won't do and I just won't do it.'

He scurried around his small town house, collecting all the things that were necessary for a nice relaxing break away from it all. But he couldn't really find anything that fitted the description of things necessary for a nice relaxing break away from it all, so he just packed some more robes, his ID documents, his crystal imaging device, so that at least he would be able to remind himself afterwards that he had had a holiday, a few pairs of scroll readers (he was always forgetting where he'd put the last pair) and a snorkel. 'Well, you never know ...' he said to himself.

There was a great urgency about this sudden need for a holiday. He told himself it wasn't there, nibbling away at his toes, like Bongadin. He hid the puzzling and immediate nature of this new turn of events, like an old pair of pyjamas shoved under the bed when they should really go in the wash but who had the time?

Breakfast, breakfast, he hadn't even had that yet! That was OK; he reassured himself that he could always eat out. He could eat on the way, in town, when he'd sorted out a ticket for somewhere or other. That was a point – maybe he should go and eat somewhere and then decide where to go. He could decide at his leisure, over a leisurely breakfast, leisurely. Yes, that was the answer. But right now was not the time to be leisurely. He needed to go.

He took one last look at his kitchen; he had turned all the meters off and plugged up the water holes and unplugged the cooking box (the box that cooked his dinners). In his washing and dressing room everything was locked down and plugged up and turned off and bolted in. There wasn't much else to do that he could think of to make the little house secure.

'Ah,' he suddenly remembered, 'leave notes for the cleaner, the launderer, the meal deliverer, the vegetable plot attendant …' (he was loath to leave his recently sown bean plants) ' … and the roof watcher' (he had had a particularly annoying set of Trashing Storks that, if not watched out for and shooed away, would nest above the windows and dribble down the panes).

The prophet busied himself with writing notes, not in his best handwriting – he was, after all, in such a great hurry – before finally slamming the door behind him.

Jonah son of Amittai took a deep breath, hiked up his backsack, pulled down his hat flaps, fastening them under his scrawny bristly chin, unlocked his scooterer, hitched up his robes and pedalled off down the street in a fury of dust and stones.

With this all-so-sudden departure, he had failed to see the handwritten note, which coincidentally held the same message delivered to him earlier that day and every day in the preceding five days by the message-bot, and which each time he had subsequently ordered to be wiped. This fresh handwritten note, which was now attached with a tiny pin to the cord of his deep, mellow, clanging doorbell, read:

'Go at once to Nineveh, that great city, and cry out against it; for their wickedness has come up before me.'

Joppa, Gateway to the Stars

Either it was further than he remembered or he was just getting on in years – whatever the cause, it was at least an hour later than he had imagined it would be before he arrived at the outer limits of the metropolis that was Joppa, Planetary Gateway to the Stars.

Breakfast long forgotten, it was most certainly lunch that now focused his thoughts. Should he find somewhere now to eat, before he caught a transporter into the centre, or should he just press on and eat when he got there? Although the stirrings of hunger were most prevalent, that deeper, inexplicable urge, which had sent him flying from home and propelled him on and on, had not abated.

Jonah paid the fee and then deposited his dusty scooterer into the property storage unit at the transporter base. He then stood in the queue to buy his one-way ticket into the city and, hitching up his robes, trotted across to the waiting vehicle in the bay. The transporters arrived and departed every quarter of an hour, so there was no real hurry, but he had just remembered and subsequently realised that he most definitely wanted to go to a particular eatery with great views out across the port, which, due to its position, was understandably popular. He didn't want to have to hang around too long to get a place.

There was quite a crowd waiting to get on the transporter – a lot of families, children and grannies and uncles and cousins, with bags packed for the day and a few makeshift flags and streamers waving around, which got in his way as he tried to clamber past them all to a quiet spot at the back of the vehicle. It was only about a ten-minute trip into the centre; Jonah frowned, realising he would now have to let them all get off first before he attempted to leave, and he hoped they weren't all heading for the same place that he was.

He flopped down into his seat, throwing his backsack on the floor at his feet, and waited for the engines to chug into life. What was the driver waiting for? There surely wasn't room for anybody else to be seated?

After what seemed like the whole ten minutes that it would have taken them to get into town, they eventually moved off and out of the parking bay, clouds of dust and steam enveloping them for just a moment before the transporter picked up speed and whisked off towards the centre of Joppa.

The buildings were remarkably bright and polished, it seemed to Jonah. There were bold banners stretched between the roof tops and at each window there was at least one flag displaying the national colours, weaving back and forth with the rush of city movement, on either side of almost every street they ran through. Sometimes the transporter just hovered at ground level, sometimes up at roof height, depending on how the traffic was or wasn't flowing. The city transporters had equal access to any level of travel within the city, as well as having priority over every other vehicle, excepting emergency call-outs of course. It was such an age since he had visited the city; they had really made an effort to smarten things up, he noticed.

Then Jonah recalled the recent news articles he had seen snapshots of, and it all made sense: Jeroboam II was doing a national tour, and by the looks of it he was due in Joppa today.

'Well, I certainly pick my moments,' he huffed to himself. There was surely going to be absolutely no room in any eatery today, let alone the one he'd set his sights on.

It was a long time since he had had anything to do with politics and a long time since he had laid eyes on the king, apart from on the news screens. It seemed that the need for a prophet was not paramount these days; such services were not much in demand – the country was tucked up in a comfortable blanket of stability and vague prosperity. Not that Jonah minded; he had after all put himself out in the sticks, in a state of semi-retirement.

'Why did I think it should be semi-retirement?' he mumbled as he stared out of the window at lots of other windows as they flew by. 'Why am I not fully retired? I could be, you know …'

From the seat in front of him, a pair of huge glassy brown eyes stared back at him. The child in front, to whom the eyes belonged, held on to the back of the seat with grubby fingers, watching him, as if poised to pounce. Jonah started and stared back. The child dipped down behind the seat. He could have smiled but he didn't feel like amusing a child, especially one that stared so rudely.

A big flashing holographic poster of Jeroboam II flickered in the air, stretching across the street in front of the transporter, appearing to shatter as they broke through it. Jonah turned back to see it materialise once more in the air space behind them; things had moved on a bit. Once he had been useful in government. Hadn't he been instrumental in the early days of satellite expansion, when they had consolidated their territory, securing Lebo Hameth and Arabah? Then he had been a prophet of standing and people had listened to his words. But that was then, and now … well, he didn't have very much to say. Perhaps he had stopped listening; perhaps it was a state of affairs that had just crept up on him, and perhaps, most of the time at any rate, he wasn't really that bothered.

For a moment the thought crossed his mind that he should have been invited to the celebrations, whatever they were. A brief pang of disappointment bubbled to the surface that he had been forgotten. But then again, would he really have wanted all that fuss and bother?

'No, I'm on my holidays and that's that,' he said to himself.

'Me too,' the big pair of brown glassy eyes replied.

Jonah scowled and waggled his hat flaps. The eyes giggled and disappeared behind the seat once more.

Most of the passengers scrambled off the transporter at the central city plaza stop, and Jonah was relieved. It looked like the main hub of ceremonial activities was going to be in and around the governmental buildings and parks, so hopefully the port would be less crowded and he could have his long-awaited meal after all. He sat back as he and the other few remaining passengers flew off round the corner, heading west.

The transporter had to jostle for position in the terminus bays; it was inordinately busy and Jonah's heart sank once more. Gathering his belongings, he made his way along the length of the vehicle, muttered his token thanks to the driver, even though it was just a driver-bot, and stood on the ground staring up at the enormous dark grey building before him that was the city port. There was no fancy array of steps to mount, which for the busy traveller would have just been a nuisance. Instead, a wall of revolving glass doors, constantly on the move, sucking people in and spitting them out, ran the length of the building at ground level.

He wondered whether he should book his ticket now or whether he should decide over a leisurely lunch. A leisurely lunch, of course, that was what he had planned. He was on holiday after all, and at last he could relax and enjoy the day.

'Now, where was that restaurant?'

He found a trolley board and plonked his backsack on it, hoping he could still remember how to use one. With one foot on the floor and one on the board, and two hands gripping the top handle for dear life, he pushed off along the road at a very refined and prophet-like pace, watching out in case the trim of his robe got trapped in the wheels.

It was a moment of dual emotion finding the restaurant. He felt elation that he'd found it – it looked wonderful, glinting in the patchy sunlight, full of culinary promise – but even though his stomach was very empty, it sank with disappointment at the bulging queue clamouring at the doors. Jonah and his trolley trundled to a sad halt, just stopping behind the crowd. Why was it so extraordinarily difficult to get away from it all?

He supposed that maybe he should go back to the port entrance and pick up some travel leaflets, because up till now he hadn't even thought about his ultimate destination – or he could simply wait in the queue.

'No, waiting will never do. I can't wait today.' He shook his head and was about to turn back when he heard a hearty voice and felt an even heartier slap on his shoulder, which nearly sent him and his trolley flying into the collective heels of the unsuspecting crowd in front.

'Jonah son of Amittai! You old dog!' This statement was followed by another slap. 'Where have you been hiding yourself? Hey, watch it, you're going to derail all those nice folks in front if you're not careful!' The owner of the hearty voice laughed an even heartier laugh.

Jonah picked himself up from near collapse and brushed himself down, retrieving his hat from under the wheels of the trolley. Looking up, he saw the ruddy face of Mr Swillows, previously Underkeeper of the LEGs (Lesser Executive Grants – a mostly ineffectual government committee, which met infrequently for tea and biscuits and not much else). He wasn't at all sure if it was a nice thing or not.

'Well … I was just here on …' Jonah began.

'Ah, come to see the celebrations, eh? Didn't get an invite, then?' Mr Swillows winked at him.

'Well … I wasn't really aware of …'

'Come on, I'll buy you lunch.' Mr Swillows wasn't to be contradicted, and most certainly not when it came to lunch.

It had, after all, worked out wonderfully well. Mr Swillows, previously Underkeeper of the LEGs, although now retired (and that being quite absolutely retired), obviously still retained some influence. In his line of work he had made all the right connections and had had lots of fingers in lots of pies – that was how government worked, everybody knew that. Prophets, however, were not quite in the same league, or did not necessarily move in the same circles. They tended to fly in and out of favour quicker than the flipping of a hot cheese Joppa pancake, invariably having little time between various bits of propheting to make the right sort of connections or to get the right number of fingers in the right number of pies.

Leading Jonah by the elbow, Mr Swillows made a way through the crowd; people let them pass by with only a momentary puzzled frown. Within minutes Mr Swillows had accosted the door manager by a measured lift of his eyebrows and they were both greeted with a nod and a bow and escorted to the best table in the house.

Things were looking up, although Jonah wished he had had time to change his robes. However, it didn't really matter, not after all that had happened up till now – all those messages, all that rushing about. He relished the moment; he was seated comfortably, the waiter was pouring him a glass of wine, he would very soon have a view out across the port buildings and beyond, and an order of steak, potatoes and spicy red sauce was on its way.

'Bottoms up!' he said, raising his glass to clink it with that of Mr Swillows, who seemed equally pleased with himself at securing the best table, and with company for a change – even if that company came in the shape of a semi-retired, dusty old forgotten prophet.

What really made this particular restaurant a cut above the rest was that it could actually be above the rest. It was one of only a few hostelries or bars that could elevate between city levels. A gentle hover-propellation engine enabled it to climb up and down between the building and transport levels, within its own pillar of space, adjacent to the main port building. As a rule it would rise and lower every hour or so, depending on the need to deposit sated paid-up guests or pick up hungry new ones to keep its tables full.

'So, you didn't get an invite to the knees-up at Government House; you just decided to come along anyway, just for old times' sake, eh?' Mr Swillows asked his table companion.

'Well, actually, I didn't really …' Jonah faltered, at the same time wondering why his lunch companion did not seem to have an invite either. Surely he should have been at Government House, wining and dining with the great tribe of civil servants. Maybe, Jonah thought and then strongly suspected, the existence of Mr Swillows and that of the LEGs committee had been so deeply buried under innumerable layers of government that they no longer registered on any list at all.

Their dazzling conversation was interrupted by a recorded announcement: 'Ladies and gentlemen, welcome to Bernie's, the best of the west in Joppa, Gateway to the Stars. We shall shortly be elevating to roof level. Please give your full attention to our safety briefing, even if you are a regular customer …'

Mr Swillows swiped his hands as if to swat a fly. 'Don't worry about all that; you've been here before, right?'

'Well, it was quite some years ago, but …' began Jonah.

'It's great to see you back. So tell me, what does an old prophet do for fun these days? Got an allotment?' laughed Mr Swillows, downing the contents of his extra-large glass.

Jonah was sure that if he'd been sitting next to him rather than across the table from him, he would have suffered another solid slap on the back. It seemed that for Mr Swillows, previously Underkeeper of the LEGs, this was not his first drink of the day.

Determined to get a word in and also determined that when he did, it would not be the word 'well', Jonah cleared his throat and launched in.

'I'm going on holiday; well, that is, I'm about to book one … and yes, I shall go on one, a holiday that is, today that is too, yes.'

Mr Swillows took a few moments to register this sudden run of words, which, although it did contain the word 'well', did not at least begin with it.

'Ah, I see,' he responded after a while. 'So you're not here to catch a glimpse of good old Jeroboam, then? Thought not.' He swallowed the remaining drops of wine in his glass and reached for the bottle. 'Between you and me, Jonah, I think he's waning.'

His glass now full to the brim once more, he continued, 'Yes, that's just the word – waning. He's had a good run; we were there, weren't we, in the good times, eh? But …' he tapped his finger against his bulbous shiny nose, 'definitely waning, know what I mean?'

Jonah wasn't too bothered either way whether their current head of state was waxing or waning. It was just a coincidence that he was here at all.

'It's just a coincidence that I'm here at all,' he told Mr Swillows. 'Oh … no, thank you. I'm fine,' he added, covering his glass with his hand as Mr Swillows waved the bottle in his direction. Having come to the conclusion that Jonah agreed with him on the waning of Jeroboam, Mr Swillows shrugged and then continued: 'So then, holiday, is it? Very nice. Off to the outer worlds, somewhere exotic? There's a great little resort I went to some years back, very natty, beautiful natives – gorgeous, know what I mean?' He winked again as he drained his glass once more. 'If you like, I can fix you up. I'm sure I've got a few numbers still.' He made a fumbling attempt to locate a notebook that was perhaps lurking in the depths of his greasy jacket pocket.

The restaurant had just reached the top elevation and was now floating, with the occasional benign waft when a transporter or spaceship passed or hovered a bit too closely, at one of the highest points in the city of Joppa. The view was far better than Jonah remembered and, ignoring everything else, he stared out of the window. Huge ships which had just entered the atmosphere were humming in their docking bays, droplets forming on their hulls while what looked like huffs of steam gusted off their noses. Although the ships were of varying sizes – liners, containers, transporters, cruisers, together with several warships – there was not one that you wouldn't describe as vast. Even in the daylight, the spectacle was stunning. Each ship had lights along the hulls or on the noses or the tails, flashing on and off, different colours, different speeds. Some of them were docking; some of them were idling away from the triangular marked-out landing zones; others were taxiing towards the flight zones; and in the distance, through the clouds, the lights of yet others could be seen as they hung in the air awaiting clearance to land.

It was indeed a sight for sore old prophet eyes and for a few moments Jonah felt excitement again. All at once a little voice in his ear spoke the message, the message he had been running away from: 'Go, go, go to the great city …'

'So where's it to be, then, this holiday of yours?' The spiny words of Mr Swillows, who had long since given up finding his notebook and was bored of the view from the window, broke into Jonah's thoughts.

'Where am I going?' Jonah sounded suddenly lost, caught out in his failure.

'Holiday.' Mr Swillows waggled his wine glass across the table at him. 'Where will it be?'

Jonah took another quick glance out of the window. He noticed a battered old green container ship just descending through the clouds on to the landing zone. He screwed up his eyes to read the flickering yellow sign running along its hull.

'Tarshish,' he blurted out.

'What! That old place? That's in the back of beyond, that is.' Mr Swillows shook his head; he was too inebriated to look more startled. 'That's no holiday destination; it's a pit, that's what that is!'

Jonah thought quickly. 'Well, there are some rather interesting historical ruins there – artefacts and the like – as it happens,' he mumbled.

Thankfully for them both, the arrival of lunch brought sweetness to a rapidly souring conversation.

With insincere promises to meet up again for a drink or two, the table companions parted company as they reached the ground level once more, a meagre half-hour after their lunch. Jonah son of Amittai had somehow or other generously paid the bill; he didn't have much else to spend his money on, and after all he was on holiday. Mr Swillows was expertly bundled into a waiting taxi by a public service-bot and passed out before he could acknowledge Jonah's final farewell. Jonah loaded another trolley with his backsack, put on his hat with its floppy ear flaps, and walked back along the road, pushing the trolley this time, until he was in sight of the wall of revolving doors that made up the main entrance to the city port.

Five minutes later, he was relieved and surprised to find that he had manoeuvred himself through the doors without major mishap, glad that he'd only had one glass of wine with lunch. He stood and stared at the desks and queues and escalators and bridges and, beyond all that, through the enormous glass walls that separated the port building from the ships themselves – some gleaming in the sunlight, some quaking in the docks, some strutting and shuddering like snorting bulls in a pen.

He began to push his trolley along, all the way along the vast hallway, past the desks and their queues on his left-hand side, with the revolving doors on his right; he was not at all sure what he was doing. Rounding a curve in the hallway, the very last desk, with absolutely no queue at all, came into sight. The possibility of going somewhere quickly, with no waiting around, was before him again. He could be away, on holiday, relaxing, enjoying life. He could disappear. The boarding over the desk read 'Tarshish Transportation Co'.

To be truthful, he was neither disappointed nor surprised; something about the place or the ship or just the name had stuck with him.

Jonah was leaving Joppa and was heading for the stars, to the far-flung satellite outpost of Tarshish.

'This is going to be a great holiday.'

From Within

Such a strange sense of gravity. I can feel it sucking us – the capsule and me – down, wherever or whichever way down is. Actually there shouldn't be any gravity, not out here in the utter middle-of-nowhere space. Whatever has eaten us for lunch must have its own energy or system, creating some sort of gravitational field … I am not the scientist here. I can only muse with a gleaned amount of general knowledge about such things. We are in the very depths of some living thing, being squeezed and throttled into sausagemeat, whilst at the same time I suppose we are floating, cast adrift in the whole great breadth that is space and the universe and beyond.

The question must be asked, and I can only ask it of myself: why did I take that passage on that ship, of all ships?

The answer must be voiced, and I alone can speak it: because it was irrelevant which ship I took, it was the fact that I took one at all, in completely the wrong direction.

Oh my word, what is that noise, that beating, booming herd of Melephantations?!

We must be sliding towards the heart of this animal! It's like wave upon ponderous wave of pulsating life. The sound, the rhythm, is like the clamour I imagine would come from a huge bell; it's enough to cause some serious damage to one's hearing!

How long will the capsule hold out against the swirling juices that surround us? How long will I hold out once the capsule has given way?

God, I am Jonah. I was once your prophet and now I am at the very end. The knowledge of you is all I have left.

And a still small voice answers: 'Jonah'.

Sheol II: Destination Tarshish

The young man at the desk was very bored – so bored, in fact, that when an old prophet came towards him, with a stupid-looking hat on and an outdated, tired backsack, he positively grinned and stood to attention; something close to interesting might be occurring. Although on second thoughts, what would somebody like him be doing coming to the Tarshish desk? Another lost soul wandering the port, looking for the exit or the toilets or the bar?

'Good afterno…' the prophet began; then, hesitating, he squinted at the hour-display above the desk to reassure himself. 'Yes, good. It is as I thought. So then, good afternoon, sir. Is it possible to book passage on …' Again Jonah halted mid-sentence and strained his neck, searching behind the desk, through the glass wall, to the visible waiting ships. 'On that ship there, please?' He pointed a wiggly finger at the mediocre, dull-bodied space bucket that he had seen earlier arriving from Tarshish. She had once been a brighter shade of green, and her bolts and panels and mechanisms had been polished and new, without a trace of space rust. However, the light years and the dark years, the heavy service on hyper-travel highways, were written all over her bodywork.

The young man at the desk laughed just for a moment, shaking his head in his eagerness to prove his superior knowledge. 'That's not a passenger cruiser, sir. The *Sheol II* is haulage. You wouldn't find that especially comfortable. Now then …' He flipped open a viewing dial showing a much larger sort of ship, a travel cruiser, which, although not glamorous (it belonged to Tarshish after all), was far smarter and altogether more suitable for paying passengers.

'Look here, sir, if you will. This is altogether more suitable for paying passengers. I could book you a passage on this for …' He fiddled about on his handheld number dial. 'Yes, for first thing tomorrow morning, no problem at all.'

There was no doubt in the prophet's mind: he did not want to go on a smart cruiser first thing in the morning. He wanted to go on that old space bucket right now. It was strange, though: he didn't know for a fact that she was leaving now, but somehow he guessed that she was and somehow he had set his heart on her. She looked like a kindred spirit.

'Thank you all the same,' Jonah replied, 'but I really want to go on that ship now. I presume she's leaving today?'

The young man frowned, shrugged and brought up the *Sheol II*'s schedule.

'Yes, she is. In one hour, when they've unloaded. But I will need to get this authorised. It's not usual, you know.'

'Will that take long? You see, I'm in a bit of a rush …' Jonah's voice tailed off as he said this and he turned away feeling slightly embarrassed. Why on earth would a semi-retired prophet like him be in a rush to get to Tarshish? He could hardly bring himself to answer that question because if he did, well then … He shook himself back into the moment and quickly repeated his earlier question: 'Will that take long?'

The man at the desk sighed and pointed to a seat along the wall that ran next to the desk. 'I'll see what I can do. Take a seat if you will, sir.'

Jonah son of Amittai waited, though not patiently, while the young man went off to sort whatever was required to be sorted in order for him, Jonah son of Amittai, to run away.

After a few minutes he finally managed to dispel the thought which yet again told him he was, in fact, running away, by watching and counting the people coming in and out of the port building, negotiating the revolving doors. It was an easily managed distraction.

Suddenly he noticed what appeared to be a post-bot manoeuvring towards him. It was obviously, he presumed, delivering post to the various desks at the port, but Jonah was a bit surprised that they didn't have a more sophisticated system for message delivery in a place such as this. It soon became clear that they did, because the message was for him and not for any staff member stood behind a desk. The post-bot halted directly before him, holding out a message screen.

'Jonah son of Amittai, post for you, sir. Please press the appropriate place on the screen to accept.'

Who ever heard of getting post at a major planetary port? Who was he, after all? He was a semi-retired prophet about to go on holiday; who would be sending him post? Jonah knew full well whom it was from and what the message would say. A great swell of panic arose in him once more, curdling his earlier delicious lunch.

Just at that moment, the young man returned and Jonah stood up, brushing the post-bot aside. It wobbled briefly on its single axis before turning and following the prophet, who was now back at the desk, leaning over the top of it, almost falling over on to the far side in an attempt to ignore the bot.

'What news, young man? Have I got a passage?'

The man stared back at Jonah, then peered around him at the post-bot, who repeated its early statement: 'Jonah son of Amittai, post for you, sir. Please press the appropriate place on the screen to accept.'

'It looks as if you've got some post, sir. I'll wait while you answer it, if you like. No hurry.'

The prophet was angry and tried to control his rising temper.

'That,' he said, throwing a narrow-eyed glance over his shoulder at the post-bot, 'is nothing to do with me. Please can you tell me, do I have passage on the *Sheol II*?'

The man behind the desk raised his eyebrows but only answered, 'Yes, sir, although …'

'Although what?' snapped Jonah.

'Although the captain would like a quick interview with you first, just to satisfy her mind, and I really must advise you to answer your post. As I'm sure you are well aware, sir, it is illegal to ignore your postal messages and in so doing you make yourself liable for a fine in excess of …'

'All right, all right!' Jonah was a semi-retired prophet after all and he could not be seen to be doing anything outside of the law.

He whirled around, shutting his eyes against the message on the screen, muttering to himself, 'I can't, I can't. It makes no sense at all. I will not go there!'

Before the post-bot could repeat its message a third time, Jonah's voice burst out in a strangled squeak, 'Wiped!' As he had done with all the others, he pressed his thumb against the screen to pay for the process, and he and the post-bot turned away from each other without any further business being conducted.

'Now then,' Jonah began, 'do I pay now or on board ship?'

The captain was waiting for him, or so it seemed, at the embarkation platform of the *Sheol II*. She was extremely tall and well built and Jonah's first thought was that she would not stand any messing about, not from anybody, not even a semi-retired prophet. The smoke from her pipe clouded around her; her long straw-matted fringe also guarded her features as she leant against the side of her ship, one leg crossed in front of the other.

With some degree of excitement about this new part of his adventure – his holiday, rather – he drew himself up, hitched his backsack securely over one shoulder and toddled towards the waiting captain.

'I think you might be waiting for me, Jonah son of Amittai, your new passenger?' He tried to sound breezy and carefree, like someone who was going on an actual holiday.

Instead of putting out a hand or saluting or making any gestures of greeting whatsoever, the captain continued smoking and, with a brief glance down at him, asked for his papers. Jonah handed them over, unperturbed by her lack of enthusiasm, and let his backsack slip off his shoulder in the hope that she would realise his semi-retired state and call for assistance perhaps, or another trolley at least. After a few minutes she swiped the papers back in his direction. He had to be quick and grab them in case she suddenly let go and they flew off into the humming engines. She continued smoking for a while.

'All in order, I presume?' he ventured, shuffling the sheets back into order before stuffing them inside his robes.

The captain uncrossed her legs and shook out her pipe, knocking it against the hull of her ship. The deeply hollow response sent an unexpected chill down his spine.

'Right …' She began talking and walking at the same time. Jonah had to follow quickly, walking in order to hear the talking. He dragged his backsack up again over his shoulder and ran after her.

'I am captain of this old nag, the *Sheol II*, or 'Sheila' as I prefer to call her, and have been for the last 15 years. There is nothing that gets past me and I know every illegal trick there is. Seen it all, done it all and paid for it all. I am aware of every bolt and screw and gravity joint there is and when they need attention and when any member of my crew is not paying attention. I have started battles and ended them. I have lost good crew and fired bad crew. The safe passage of my ship is the only thing I care about and this is not a free ride …'

At this point Jonah ventured an interruption. 'Yes, I know, I have paid already' was what he intended to say but all he managed to squeeze into the conversation was, 'Y…'

Unheeding, she continued, 'As I said, this is not a free ride. Everyone works for their passage.'

At this point Jonah son of Amittai thought he had heard enough and he really ought to stand up for himself. He stopped, hoping that she would stop too.

'I am semi-retired – a prophet, you know!' he shouted after her retreating figure.

She did stop and turn around, giving him another swift glance up and down before saying, 'Report for kitchen duties in 30 minutes.' Then she stomped away in her big boots, as casual as any captain could ever be.

'Well …' Jonah let his sack fall to the ground once more. He was lost for words, but then he did manage to find a few: 'Well …' again and then, 'I have never …' Then he managed, 'How can …' and then, 'I really do think …' and lastly, 'Well …'

It only took a few minutes for him to realise that he had no idea where he was.

The embarkation platform must have been raised with them both on board while she was viewing his papers, which he hadn't noticed. Then she had walked off inside the ship, with him following. This was indeed some holiday. He stopped himself thinking any more about what he had chosen and decided that the sensible thing to do was to find some sort of reception desk or information point or something. Find where he had been designated a berth and, 'Well,' he added to himself, 'I suppose I had better then locate the kitchens.'

At first he followed the gloomy corridor along which the captain had gone. Although she had seemed totally unhurried and unexcited about the trip (she had been doing it for many years, after all), she had long legs and had completely disappeared from view, even though it looked as if the corridor was one long length, probably the whole length of the ship.

Jonah shuffled along, peering at any signs he saw or any doorways. All was dark and surprisingly quiet.

'Jonah son of Amittai, this way, please.' A light broke out above a certain doorway, which opened as he approached. The light revealed a tiny cabin with a bunk on each side, a couple of lockers and a washing unit at the back. He stepped inside the cabin and looked at the bunks; they both appeared to be the same, untouched, so he lifted his backsack, ready to throw it on top of the right-hand-side one.

'Jonah son of Amittai, not that one, the other one,' said the voice again.

There was no one around but it felt like a trick. He threw his sack across on to the left-hand-side bunk and looked up into all the corners for signs of a camera or speaker or something. He couldn't detect a thing. He was so tired. To say it had been a rather busy day was, in his understanding, an understatement. He sat on the bunk, next to his sack, and lay down, bringing his legs up. As he shut his eyes the commanding voice spoke again: 'Jonah son of Amittai, you have 15 minutes to rest. Then report to the kitchens. Door 315, level four.'

'315 … level four …' Jonah murmured to himself as he shut his eyes once more.

Waking suddenly from what seemed like a whole night of sleep, it felt like everything was happening at once. It had in actual fact been just the prescribed 15 minutes, but an alarm was sounding, the walls were shuddering, the bunk was jittering across the floor and the speaker was spewing commands out at him. Jonah sat on the edge of his dancing bunk and tried to gather his thoughts.

'Jonah son of Amittai, your time is up.'

'What?' he called back out into the dimly lit room.

'Jonah son of Amittai, report to the kitchens.'

'Report to the what? Oh yes. 315, level four.' He finally remembered where he was.

'Attention all crew: the *Sheol II* is about to take flight. Please ensure your safety headgear and clothing are correctly in place about your person.'

'What? What headgear?' Jonah frantically looked around him.

'Please ensure all baggage is safely stowed away in the personal lockers and report to the sub-bridge for briefing. Any failure to do so will result in a first-level penalty. Thank you for your attention.'

The voice finally ceased shouting commands but the alarm still seemed to be sounding. The shaking ship was rattling its way through the atmospheric blanket above Joppa, holding its own against a notoriously heavy gravitational pull, although significant grating and rumbling sounds and movements told a different story.

Jonah stood, tentatively at first, and found that he did not seem to slide around as much as he'd feared he would. Somewhere in the back of his mind he knew that time was of the essence and he tried to think clearly. The lockers seemed well and truly locked, so he stuffed his backsack under the bed, where it held, satisfactorily wedged. He searched for headgear and clothing that might fit the bill of 'safety' headgear and clothing. On the back of the door hung a sort of overall one-piece in navy blue. It would not fit over his robes, and a prophet should always wear his robes without question, even when faced with dragons or a firing squad or reckless peril in space, and even when semi-retired. So Jonah decided to wear his robes over this overall outfit, thus fulfilling both requirements, he hoped, to everyone's satisfaction. As for headgear, there was a skullcap with an attached earphone device in the pocket of this overall. Peering at the earpiece, which didn't seem particularly clean, he decided to perch the cap on top of his own hat (the one with the earflaps), which was a much more comfortable option.

As if someone was watching his every move, the door opened as soon as he had got himself ready and the voice stated, 'Safety briefing, sub-bridge, level one. *Then* proceed to kitchens – 315, level four.'

Jonah stood outside the door, looking in both directions. There was a sudden roaring from the ship's engines as it finally broke through the atmosphere and swerved off, away from the nearest orbiting routes and out into open space. All was quiet – well, not 'quiet' in the sense of no noise but 'quiet' in the sense of nobody about. He had expected and he had indeed hoped to see a crowd of smart but tough crew members scurrying in one direction or another, but the corridor was empty. He started to move off in the direction that wasn't the one he had originally come from, when earlier he had followed the captain, but no sooner had he stepped out that way, which was to the left of the door, than the voice spoke again. 'Jonah son of Amittai, not that way.'

Just to himself, because he thought that somebody would probably be listening, he muttered, 'I'm getting a little bit tired of this voice.' He waited for a response and decided that whoever it was that was listening had either not heard his comment or decided they were above responding. Setting out back along the corridor, which did at first seem nonsensical, he hit a junction that certainly hadn't been there before – well, at least he didn't think it had. Directly in front of him was what looked like a lift, with a small sign which read, 'Lift to sub-bridge, use at your own risk.'

Without a second thought he pressed the button underneath and, in less than half a minute, the lift door opened. It was enormous, the size of a vast lobby, and absolutely jam-packed full with red-eyed, scruffily shaven, drooling, lopsided, scar-faced crew members.

'Room for a small one …?' he inquired in the tiniest voice he could manage, which wasn't difficult as they were a pretty menacing-looking lot, and at that moment he would have given anything to have the doors close swiftly between them.

Nobody said a word in response; nobody moved a muscle, apart from the one guy in the front who continued slowly chewing whatever it was he had already been chewing when the door first opened, and another somebody who blinked, just the once. Jonah didn't move either and was just about to say something along the lines of 'Oh well, I'll get the next one …' when somebody growled, 'You getting in or not? We're late.'

Gathering his robes, which did look rather silly (he had never thought that before about his robes, that in certain situations they could indeed look silly), Jonah squeezed into the immovable mob. The doors snapped shut, catching the edge of his robes in their teeth, and then the lift plummeted, he could only assume, into the depths of the ship, which was strangely where he thought he had been before, back in the cabin. The motion sent his skullcap shooting off from its precarious position, up into the unknown darkness of the lift above their heads.

As sub-bridges went, this wasn't too bad, he thought as the lift doors opened on to a sort of deck area, twice as big again as the size of the lift. As he was right at the front of the crowd, he had no choice but to head straight forward on to the deck to face the captain once again. (Well, of course he did have a choice – something which he himself was always purporting to great effect – he could have walked straight out as he had chosen to do or he could have stayed where he was and been trampled to death. It was still a choice, of sorts.)

At least he could breathe a bit more freely here on the sub-bridge; personal hygiene, he had very recently come to realise, was not high on the agenda for this motley crew.

There was the captain in all her no-nonsense splendour; however, there was also the most tremendous view, which reached through the wide screen before him, and unfortunately for Jonah he spent the next 20 minutes or so staring out at the stars ahead, below, above and all around them. Their formations were things he had seen before, on occasion and in books, but it had been a very long time since he had been this far out in space and he got quite excited thinking that their journey was only just beginning. They were travelling to Tarshish of all places, as far out as you could get, at least with a local constellation visa.

Nevertheless, all this stargazing did indeed prove to be unfortunate because he missed nearly everything the captain had to say.

'So then, I hope you are all familiar with your roles, come that eventuality.' She was finishing up now, having briefed them all on the proposed changes to the emergency procedures in light of possible route alterations based on unspecified reports of unsettled space configurations.

'We will be thrusting out into hyperspace in a few hours' time, when we have cleared the major routes, so remember your positions. Breakfast will begin for the first shift in three hours' time. Dismissed.'

Scrawny, reckless-looking crew-hands flew off, everyone in a different direction. Appearances were deceptive: they knew exactly what they were doing, each and every one of them, all except Jonah.

He was left standing alone on the sub-bridge, the captain's towering figure silhouetted against the stars.

'I am a prophet, semi-retired but nonetheless a prophet. I shouldn't be involved in all this.' He looked around for a comfortable chair.

'You, prophet-man, kitchens!' someone whispered in his ear, but it wasn't the sort of whisper that made you feel special. Jonah took off, away from the voice, which laughed after him, 'Watch ya don't spoil your dress, fancy boy.'

If he had felt any stronger he would have turned back and put that person straight on the matter of dresses and robes, but he had a kitchen to find.

He should have realised that the kitchens would be easy to find. Just follow your nose. There was a great brewing, broiling sort of smell that drew him along yet another corridor. It was quite the sort of smell that would have been really good if you were starving and on a budget, but not so good if you'd just got paid and were out celebrating a promotion perhaps or your Great-Aunt Delilah's birthday.

Steam burst through a pair of doors in front of him as they swung open and shut, and great shouts and clangs and bangs of all descriptions told him that he was heading in the right direction. Sadly he knew he would be far too hot and hoped they could find him something simple like chopping fresh herbs or washing lettuces.

Inside the swinging doors a three-armed person was growling at him, though he couldn't understand a word of it. Then it dawned on him that there would naturally be a whole host of different languages and cultures represented on such a vessel, and that the mucky earpiece he had left hanging on the skullcap was in fact most probably a translating device. His cap (at least he hoped it was his cap) had thankfully come back to rest once more on his head after the initial lurch in the lift, and so Jonah retrieved the earpiece, gave it a quick wipe and stuck it in his ear.

'… You stupid great idiot' (and a few more choice, untranslatable words), 'get yourself moving! That Bringjom is already half out of its pan! I need it up to temp in ten, yesterday!'

The earpiece worked and now Jonah understood exactly what the three-armed chef had meant when he or she (not always easy to tell) had been shouting and gesticulating between himself, the prophet and the pan on the stove.

The pan on the stove was almost as big as his cabin and there were already two other crew members fighting with the tentacled creature, amid flames and steam and tongs and prongs, to subdue the Bringjom and get it quietly into the pan, with the lid firmly on. For obvious reasons this creature was not going down without a fight and the services of a semi-retired prophet were now called upon to help in that fight. Jonah threw off his robes and dived into battle; he was, by now, long past questioning or wondering how or why or what he was doing on the *Sheol II*, headed for Tarshish.

From Within

'Jonah, hear me, hear me, I am calling to you in the great deep place where you are. I have not banished you; you have banished yourself and have run from me. But you are always in my sight, always just a breath away from my mercy; even here at the end of everything where you could slip away into nothingness, I am here with you.'

That voice, I know that voice. There have been so many voices but this is the one that I know and that knows me. I had forgotten what it was to listen.

Oh God, my God, I feel as if waters of death are squeezing me and sucking me into just fragments of a man. All this churning and these waves that seem to be pushing me, breaking the capsule around my head – I am being utterly engulfed by this mountain of a creature, I am slipping down into the core of its very being.

I do remember you, my Lord, I do, I do.

Besides you there is nothing worth clinging to; nothing else has so much love and grace. Whether I live or die now in this black hole, I am thankful to have known you, and what I promised long ago will never leave me. I am yours.

Why did I ever think it could be otherwise?

Levantine, the Comet's Tail

Jonah's respect for chefs and all who worked in kitchens, generally, had gone up quite a few notches. He also now had a far greater appreciation of the delicacy that was Bringjom soup, and he sat in a corner of the kitchen actually feeling something close to satisfaction. The soup had indeed been good, always a favourite on board ship, but having tackled the dish himself, quite literally, the savour was somehow all the sweeter. He had been hoping to slip away after his meal, but just as he was finishing up, the same three-armed chef accosted him with a ladle round his earflaps, and directed him towards the washing-up. Normally this would have made the jolliest person's heart sink, let alone Jonah son of Amittai's. However, with a full stomach his heart couldn't sink very much further and he gathered himself and his robes, which he was now carrying around in a bundle due to the excessive heat and steam in the kitchens, and headed off to find the washing-up.

The washing-up was, as it ever was, a monotonous job. He had heard, through distant rumouring, that the monotony made it therapeutic, but he had never before found it to be true, so now, he thought, was his chance. So far, this holiday was proving to be a little more challenging than Jonah had expected, but he was not deterred. He had blended with the crew, to a certain extent; he had not been beaten up yet, apart from a ladle round his earflaps; he had made his way around the ship, albeit unwittingly, and he had triumphed in the soup pan, so he was more than ready for the next challenge.

There was a doorway with a sign which read 'Washing-up only – please wear appropriate clothing'. He could not see any appropriate clothing so he opened the door anyway. This was a mistake. Quickly retreating amid shouts and swearing and vicious blasts of steam, in his momentarily sightless state he felt himself being roughly escorted towards another doorway, just to the left of the washing-up door, with a sign that read 'Appropriate clothing'. Once he had been pushed inside this next door, his head began to clear and he found that he had not been permanently blinded after all, although his eyebrows seemed to have diminished in size. (Some would have said that it suited him better that way.)

There were goggles and gloves and voluminous all-in-one waterproof suits. The difficulty lay in the robes once more. He couldn't carry them with him and he couldn't find anywhere to stash them, so he decided to put them on again over his overalls and under this new plastic suit. Emerging from the 'Appropriate clothing' door, he waddled back to the 'Washing-up' door and attempted once more to acquire a new skill.

An hour had passed by but it felt like only five minutes. He couldn't say he was enjoying himself, that would be far too rash, but he realised that he had not had time to talk to himself or to think, and, given his circumstances, he decided that wasn't a bad thing. He had, however, had time to grapple with the huge swimming-pool that was the washing-up sink. Great tracks suspended in the steaming water rolled endlessly through the depths, dipping in and out, to be sprayed with detergent or squirted with steam blasts, which was what had caught him out earlier. The job of the washer-upper was to load and unload the tracks, and sometimes get into the 'sinks' themselves to reload any deserting crockery or cutlery. The greatest difficulty was in stopping himself floating off down the tracks due to his huge size – not that anyone could call him a large prophet, by no means, but rather due to his many layers of apparel. Several times even within that first hour, other washer-uppers had had to jump in and rescue him from the central swirling plug hole.

Although he had not been talking to himself, he had been conversing a little with his fellow crew; a little friendly banter had passed between them after he had been rescued for the umpteenth time, and this had led to questions such as, 'What do you think you're playing at, you great lump of lard?' and 'Who gave you the job? Didn't think we were that desperate?' Those were just the mentionable ones; the rest he thought he'd probably not heard correctly, or perhaps the translator-device had been affected by the steam. At the end of the first hour, the plastic-suited crew sat out on the side of the sinks along some benches, just to catch their breath.

One of them nudged Jonah in the ribs, and, as he happened to be sitting on the end of a bench, he of course fell off. After the laughter had died down, the one who'd nudged him lifted up his goggles for a moment (the steam blasters were busy at the other end of the sink) and had a closer look at Jonah. The significance of his now more apparent maturity and other details, like the collar of his prophet's robes poking out through the hood of his plastic suit, seemed to dawn on the nudger.

''Ere, so you be a priesty, then. Many be the apologisinations, mister priesty old guy,' he said in broad Tarshishian.

Jonah attempted to laugh it off as all in good fun. 'Yes, yes. Please don't be alarmed, and actually I am a prophet not a priest. There is a difference, you know.' He smiled under his goggles, which made him look a touch malevolent, although he was rather hoping that it would show he had no hard feelings and was quite a friendly sort of chap.

'Prophety guy, ah, we sees now very muchness,' said the nudger, although he didn't really see the difference at all and was not the slightest bit interested in finding it out either. Instead he said, 'Prophety guy or priesty guy, you be still very many old years on *Sheila II*, to be activating with proper crewy guys, like us-us.' He nudged Jonah again, this time far more respectfully. 'Why you be hereness, why you tripping now with us-us?'

It was a bit like talking to himself, Jonah thought, chatting with this nudger. He didn't seem to really understand, so it didn't really matter what he told him.

'Why am I here? What a question! I am here because I am running away.' There, he had said it, out loud. It was somewhat strange.

The nudger quickly turned around, looking one way and then the other. He frowned. 'Here be no running away fromness? Who be? What be?'

'Oh no, you are quite correct, it is quite safe here on the ship for me, for us-us, as you put it.' Jonah leaned in a bit closer to the nudger. 'It's God.' He thought that would probably be enough of an explanation.

'Ah,' replied the nudger, looking none the wiser. 'God be not hereness?'

Jonah was suddenly stumped. The futility of his evasion flashed through his mind; even this humble Tarshishian did not doubt the omnipresence of a higher being. In answering, he resorted to his usual, 'Well … not exactly …'

A bell sounded for the next lot of washing-up to be commenced, and this time the nudger helped Jonah up from the bench, now that he realised what an old prophety guy he was. He suggested that Jonah go and operate the steam blaster, as that might not involve so much floating away down the plate tracks and subsequent rescuing; at least he could sit at the operating seat, and all he had to do was just press a button and aim.

There was a significant amount of water displacement and unexpected heat during that second washing-up session, and it was unanimously agreed that Jonah would not be working the steam blaster again on that trip.

'Please note, as mentioned in my earlier briefing, the Levantine comet will be passing ahead of us within the next hour. Any member of the crew wishing to witness this unusual and spectacular display must have the correct clearance from their crew manager. Any member of the crew caught watching out of their designated work area without clearance will be charged with extra penalty points.'

The captain signed off; she was not too bothered about viewing the comet herself – she had seen many a heavenly happening in her time – but she was not so hard-hearted as to deprive others. With her booted feet crossed and slung up over the rail of the main bridge, she sipped her fresh cup of the blackest Joppa Java and thought about how she might answer the company's request that she take early retirement at the end of this trip. It was not a pleasant thought but it would probably be a case of jump or be pushed. 'Cutbacks …' she swore under her breath. The idea of going solo, using her company payout to buy a small cruiser or transporter, did have its appeal, but she wasn't quite ready for doing tourist trips around some long-lost satellite, not yet.

'Sir …' All captains were referred to as such, regardless of gender. The cheeky navigator was actually interrupting her reverie; this had better be good, she thought.

'Sir, there seems to be a slight problem.'

Jonah son of Amittai was the most exhausted a semi-retired prophet-cum-commis-chef-cum-washer-upper could possibly be. He wondered how long this trip would actually last. It was a question he had forgotten to ask when he'd bought his ticket; it hadn't seemed important at the time. He emerged from the great lift, hoping it had spewed him out on the correct level, and shuffled along, his plastic suit half hanging off and dragging on the corridor floor behind him. He stopped by the first door he came to and looked up to see if it would light up or speak to him; he had no idea which cabin was his. Nothing happened, so he wandered on some more and stopped by another one and then another one. He was about to slump to the floor, thinking that he could just sleep in the corridor – he was sure no one would mind – when a light came on just a yard further down the corridor and the voice spoke: 'Jonah son of Amittai, just a little further.'

He started up again and, with one last spurt of energy, he threw himself through the waiting open door and on to the bunk.

'Not that one,' announced the voice.

Jonah rolled off the wrong bunk, on to the floor, and didn't get any further.

The slight problem on the bridge was now turning into a real emergency. Once apparently lackadaisical senior staff on the bridge were all at once milling around, taking readings, shouting out coordinates, radioing flight centres, contacting company on-call management and generally earning their money for a change. The Levantine comet that only ever passed once in a blue moon – that being the actual blue moon phenomenon of this particular part of the constellation – seemed to be violently off course. The captain knew that her Sheila wasn't; of that she was absolutely sure – they had checked and double-checked everything. But the natural course of things could not always be checked or double-checked or explained; this comet looked as if it was doing its own thing and the *Sheol II* was about to be right in its way.

The captain set everyone to work before she made her announcement. The incessant sound of a demanding alarm was now trilling throughout the ship.

'They will not be able to put me out to pasture if we get through this in one piece,' she muttered under her breath. 'If …'

She cleared her throat: 'Attention all crew members. A state of emergency is now in place. This is not a drill. I repeat, this is most definitely not a drill.'

She took a breath and then launched into a full and thorough communication about who should be doing what, how and when. There was no need to mention that failure to do so would mean penalty points; they were beyond that now. This was the most dangerous position she could remember ever being in, and the fear that her beloved Sheila would not make it was crawling around in her belly like a ladle full of very bad Bringjom soup.

The light from the comet particles was now blinding, and the first rush of ice particles began to batter the hull as the comet's tail, inexplicably on collision course with the *Sheol II*, started to hit. This tail was no miniature belt of asteroids that could be skirted around with some fancy piece of navigating. It was a vast stretch of ice and boulders and gas that filled the space between them and the rest of the universe. It was all happening far too early and far too much and in the wrong place entirely.

The shudders of the ship did not touch the sleeping semi-retired prophet. His snores were deep and mellow, and if he'd been awake to hear them he would have soundly approved; it was the well-earned sleep of good honest toil. The fact that he was actually really a prophet (although of course semi-retired), and not a real member of a hardworking, rough-necked haulage crew, had escaped him. In his escaping, the reality of who he was and what he should really be about had also escaped him.

'You, prophet man!' The captain couldn't think of anything more polite to call him. 'How can you sleep?'

His shoulders were being rubbed by an over-friendly Bringjom, whom he was trying to teach how to use a knife and fork. A rather difficult tentacled minute passed by before he realised that he was climbing out of a dream and, in reality, his shoulders were being prodded and poked by the captain's left boot.

'Well, this is an unexpected surprise …' he began.

The captain took a deep breath and repeated her earlier question, as she was sure he had not heard her the first time, judging from his murmurings about forks and suckers and slime.

'How can you sleep? The whole ship is breaking up!'

He sat up and felt the lurching and heard the crashing and sensed that there was indeed a problem. He scratched his head and rubbed his eyes. He was not a pilot or an engineer, so what on earth did she think he was going to do?

'I'm not a pilot or an engineer,' he told her. 'What is going on? I'm not going back to the kitchens, if that's what you think, not until I've had some proper training in using a steam blaster …' At this point the ship took a major hit and the captain was thrown across him. The prophet was beginning to be extremely concerned about what was really happening.

They had no time to waste and she told him so: 'Get yourself and your fancy robes up off that floor and on to my bridge. There is something we need to discuss, and I mean NOW!'

The captain half dragged him, half carried him towards the lift, his plastic suit long since fallen by the wayside. With each sideways thrust of the ship, as the *Sheol II* took her blows, they fell across the corridor and finally into the lift itself, which was now a huge empty hall with only the two of them quite literally rattling around inside it.

'I understand there is a bit of an emergency …' yelled Jonah as they slid away backwards again from the lift doors, which had already shut behind them. 'But … I fail to see how I can be of …' (he waited while they crashed back forwards again into the doors) ' … of any assistance!' He could hardly make himself heard above the noise.

The captain grabbed him by the collar of his robes, although it was not quite clear whether that was from anger or desperation or just the need to hold on to something.

'Get up on that bridge,' she was almost spitting in his face, 'and call on your god! Maybe he will take a bit of notice of us and maybe, just maybe, we will not DIE!'

Oh dear, thought Jonah, he did not realise it was as bad as all that.

'Well …' he said, brushing himself down before the next hit, 'I am a prophet, after all. I suppose this is what we do, when the necessity arises … although I am semi-retired, you know.'

The doors opened and the captain pulled Jonah across the sub-bridge, then across a narrow walkway and on to the main bridge, which had a much closer view of the universe – if the universe had been there to see, that is. It was still there, of course, but it was completely hidden by the storm of ice and rock and gas that was the Levantine comet's tail. They would have all been blinded if the screen through which they were watching everything had not been in complete shadow mode; on the other hand, the spectacle would have been amazingly beautiful if they hadn't been right in it, or if the tail had been made of something like candy floss.

Gathered on the main bridge were all the different heads and managers, who were, like the rest of the crew there, either strapped down, belted up or hanging on for dear life. Several of them had been vomiting. There was already a crack or two in the main screen through which they viewed everything. They had lost all contact with any other ship in the vicinity and with any planetary base for light years around. Only one engine was working and the lift from which they had recently emerged now had an 'out of action' sign flashing above it. Even to a semi-retired prophet it did not look good.

'Well, I must say, captain, this is a dreadful mess!' announced Jonah.

'You're telling me!' She glared at him just for stating the obvious, then switched on her micro-speaking device.

'Right,' the captain's voice rang out through the speakers. If there was any announcing to be done on board ship, she was the one to do it. 'Right. As I see it, we are probably not going to make it through this.'

The general hubbub of shock was utterly drowned by the next hit they took.

'There is one course of action left. We will put all the information we have into the ship's old predictorial device – and before anybody asks, yes, we still have one on board this vessel. Sheila may be an old girl but she still has a trick or two up her sleeve.'

The captain staggered over to an end panel next to the navigator's control desk and ripped open the cover. Sure enough, there was an ancient piece of early space travel equipment, long forgotten and covered in dust. An eye scan of every manager detailed on board ship was requisite to complete the calculations. It was a job and a half to get them all, given the unpredictability of the ship's movements, but finally they were done. The captain, sweating with concentration under such extreme circumstances, typed in as much information as she could about said extreme circumstances while they all waited, daring to believe that their last hope was about to be revealed.

'What?' Suddenly the captain looked up from the device and stared directly at Jonah. 'Him?'

She looked back at the calculator and then again at Jonah.

'It says it's him!' This time she pointed, her voice high to the point of screeching. 'It's his fault! All of this, his fault!'

Jonah son of Amittai sensed a sudden need to escape, to run away, to not be there on that bridge. Then again, wasn't that what he had already done, and wasn't that now proving to be, in fact, the worst thing he had ever done?

All at once they were all shouting at him.

'Tell us, are you responsible for this?'

'Who are you?'

'What do you do?'

'Where are you from?'

'Who are your people?'

'What did you do to make all this trouble for us?'

Jonah snatched the speaker from the captain, who was too startled to object, and began to explain, or at least to answer their questions.

'I am a prophet, a prophet of the God of heaven, who made everything, the planets and the stars and all of space and this comet, and ...'

Another crack appeared in the screen and the ship shouldered another wave of shaking.

' ... I have been running away.'

All at once, he knew it – he felt it. It had been the most stupid, most dangerous, most utterly ridiculous thing that anyone had ever done. He had once imagined that what his God had been asking him to do was the most stupid, most dangerous, most utterly ridiculous thing to do. It had not dawned on him until now that he had got it completely the wrong way round. Now, in the bracing light of destruction, it all made sense.

They were all shouting again and the captain's nose was almost touching his.

'What should we do to make this all go away?'

Jonah thought for a moment: her eyes were really pretty when she was this angry, although imagine living with someone this angry all the time, just to enjoy their beautiful eyes …

He shook himself back into the moment, with a bit of help from another hefty rock of ice hitting the screen, and focused his mind. It didn't take long; he was still a prophet, after all.

'Throw me out. Throw me off the ship.'

Pcaethon, the Bony-Finned Asteroid Fish

'I know that if you throw me off the ship, the ice storm will stop. Everything is my fault. So go ahead.' Jonah held out his hands: he expected they would want to grab him immediately and push him out of the nearest waste chute, and he didn't want to make it any more difficult for them by running away again. That had not proved to be a reasonable solution thus far.

Strangely enough, he didn't feel too worried about it all. He had, until recently, lived a useful and vaguely interesting life and, as far as he was aware, he had not caused any other real catastrophes (apart from the incident in the city hall toilets, but that was years ago and arguably not absolutely his fault). As a prophet he had fulfilled most tasks to the best of his ability. However, the truth of the matter was that on this, the final hurdle, he had failed – come unstuck, baulked, disintegrated, chickened out, fled. Therefore he could face his most imminent demise with at least the knowledge that it was a fair deal, and if the ship was saved, then all to the good.

'Absolutely not!' roared the captain.

She turned on her heel and strode with as much composure as she could, given the reeling behaviour of her ship, back towards the screen. There she began to exchange thoughts with the navigator, who was clinging to the back of his chair with one hand while scrabbling for a hold on the controls with the other. Whichever way she turned, it was impossible. What difference would one death make to the rest of them? They were all going to die, so to waste time on trying to kill him first was pointless. She didn't really believe in God, in a God that made everything, or in any other sort of god or gods. She believed in herself and her skill and experience as a captain, and she believed in her beloved ship, and to some extent she believed in her crew, most of the time, on a good day. But here was this little old prophet man, in his idiotic robes, with his bushy eyebrows (that now looked oddly singed), totally unsuited for any sort of anything in the real practical world she lived in. He hitched a lift on her ship and now they have disaster. It was just not logical that it could all be his fault, but … but … but …

'Sir, I think we should consider,' the head engineer called across to the captain, 'I think we should consider that it might be worth a try – throwing him out, I mean?'

A sudden fist of ice shards pelted towards the screen, piercing the shield, fixing themselves there like a thousand barbs. Everybody had ducked with elbows high against the expected attack. But still the screen held. The *Sheol II* was sucked sideways into the fiercest part of the tail, becoming one with the unstoppable force.

'Sir, we are now completely off course!' yelled the navigator. 'There is no way she can hold out against this.'

'You have to try!' The captain's teeth were gritted; she clung on to the rail that had just saved her from falling backwards over the walkway, all the way down to the bottom levels. 'We have never been outmatched by anything! We can get through this!'

'Captain, there is nothing left to give. Everything is finished!'

Jonah son of Amittai was somehow still standing upright, all alone it seemed, behind her on the sub-bridge. Everyone else had been thrown around like pebbles in a straining sieve, their restraints having either snapped or stretched into a condition next to useless. The captain crawled towards him until she was on her knees at his feet. She looked up at him and then fell forward, her arms curled up around her head. He heard her mumbling and moaning and he began to think that she had finally, along with the ship, lost everything:

'Do not hold us accountable for killing an innocent man … O Lord, you have done what you wanted … Please do not let us all die!'

He waited for a moment to see what would happen next. He did not have a clue where the nearest exit was, so he couldn't exactly throw himself off the ship.

With the help of the nearest few conscious and still able-bodied seniors she could muster, the captain bundled Jonah into her own personal emergency capsule, which was located right underneath her seat of command. She had always wondered why a captain should have her own escape pod when she was of the 'captain-goes-down-with-the-sinking-ship' brigade; she would never have dreamt of using it herself.

The capsule was now squashed full of prophet and he had gone in without a fight. She looked down at his small, wrinkly, red face and felt a kind of sorrow, before he wiggled a little finger free and slid the little viewing panel shut.

At the last minute, she thought maybe there was another way; maybe they could save him and save them all; maybe she just hadn't thought it through properly – she had just missed something, something they had overlooked but something vital. An odd sense of panic at the responsibility for his little life overwhelmed her. Until Jonah himself pressed the button, which ejected the capsule from the ship, she was on the point of dragging him out again.

In the rush of the icy comet's tail, amid the onslaught of rock and frozen gases, the tiny capsule was shed like the runt of the litter, left to fend for itself.

There were real tears on her cheeks as she watched the prophet-stuffed capsule disappear, not because she was going to miss him or anything sentimental like that – it was perhaps more to do with her own sense of failure. What utter desperation had caused her to make that sort of decision?

Her tears, however, were very swiftly wiped away due to the unaccountable fact that the comet and the storm of ice they had been battling through had just gone. The vicious icy tail had vamoosed, disappeared, skidaddled. The *Sheol II* was all at once waiting in stillness and darkness, floating like a piece of battered driftwood in the wake of a passing tidal wave.

The captain scrambled across to the navigator's desk, demanding an explanation.

He just looked back at her, shook his head and shrugged his shoulders. 'I ... just don't ... I don't know what's happened. It's gone.'

'Let me see!' She yanked the control panel towards her. He was right. The only sign that there had ever been a comet was a speedily retreating blur of shining crystals across their main viewing screen. There was nothing else left to see except a slowly meandering belt of asteroids far away below them, which must have been there all the time, just hidden by the comet, which now wasn't there at all. Of the capsule there was no sign whatsoever.

How in the name of all the gods in space was she going to explain this?

Jonah son of Amittai shut his eyes as soon as he had shut the viewing plate. It had all been quite calm really and, for a death sentence, well he couldn't have imagined a better send-off. Naturally they – that being himself and the crew of the *Sheol II* – hadn't had time for flags and banners, for last rites or a last meal or even a fond farewell. That would, of course, have been slightly odd, seeing as he had only just met them and could be forgiven for saying that actually he hardly knew them. However, despite the lack of all the above, it had, he thought, gone pretty well.

He wasn't really sure what to expect on being dispatched into open space like this. Having obviously never experienced it before, he had nothing by which to gauge it. At first there had been a slight slipping sensation as, he presumed, the capsule had been expelled. Then, instead of a sudden icy death as he was ripped to shreds by the comet's tail, there was a complete nothingness. He felt nothing in particular and heard nothing in particular and was just about to slide open the viewing hatch to see if there was the same amount of particular nothingness to see, when suddenly all that nothingness changed.

He heard it and felt it at the same time. To say it went darker inside the capsule was not quite accurate because it was already pretty dark inside, but it did seem to get suddenly even more so, darker than it was before, along with a cavernous, blowing, belching kind of sound that rumbled down the length of the capsule.

'Ah,' he said to himself, 'perhaps I have, after all, been swept up in the ice storm and this is the beginning of the end.' He wasn't disappointed, not entirely, because this was what he had asked for. He had expected death but it hadn't come straight away, just a bit delayed.

Although his knowledge of what he termed an ice storm was limited, somehow he wasn't convinced that this was really where he was. The sounds were much more biological than astronomical and the capsule seemed to be gently rocking about as if something or someone were rolling it over their tongue, to taste and see if it was good. 'Ah,' he said to himself, 'perhaps I have, after all, *not* been swept up in the ice storm and this is the beginning of another end altogether.'

Jonah knew that there were a lot of things out there, where he now was, that were living somehow in the vacuum of space, and that they might prey on unsuspecting emergency escape capsules. His suspicions were confirmed when he heard and felt significant humming noises which, in his experience, usually tended to indicate the fact that someone was enjoying a particular culinary delicacy. He was a sorry prophet, crammed into a discarded emergency escape capsule, which was now inside the mouth of something else entirely. Then, just as he managed to crack open the viewing plate, there was a brief moment when he thought he might be choking the creature, as harsh gusts came up from underneath the capsule in chugging, breaking motions – and suddenly he knew that he and the capsule had been swallowed.

All at once the recollection of a recent article sharply intruded on to the scene, filling his bewildered mind with trivial facts and seemingly irrelevant information …

The Bony-Finned Asteroid Fish, otherwise known as Pcaethon, is one of the few varieties of space-dwelling creature, in this galaxy at least. Until fairly recently there has been very little documented information on the habits and activities of this creature. A specially commissioned team, however, have just completed six years of monitoring and research, winning them some acclaim and standing in their field. The fish's preferred habitat is the asteroid belt (some say that it doesn't take a funded research team to tell you that), especially the smaller, less inhabited ones, where earlier mining and subsequent settlements are now either obsolete or non-existent.

In the past the Pcaethon were hunted by nomadic travellers from a variety of planets and have therefore decreased in number, especially considering, as the team discovered, that they only mate once a lifetime and a lifetime is just about six years, more or less. Their great size lends them the appearance of a great age but this apparently is not the case.

The team also discovered (and here, it could also be said, needlessly) that they have an array of bony fins running the length of their spines (of which they have two) and that it is these tough, bony fins that give them the power to 'swim', as it were, between the asteroids, against any tide of gravitational pull that might force them away and into orbit around any planet they might happen to pass.

The one thing the team did discover that nobody else could have foreseen (except, perhaps, the old nomadic hunters whose records happen to be freely available in any public information department) was the fact that the Pcaethon's diet consists almost purely of dry-red algae, which they filter through a curtain of soft, bristly teeth. The team were able to record the softness after one tooth was accidentally broken off during a measuring expedition, in which they were attempting to count the teeth. The tooth was subsequently transported back to the research base and was prodded and poked until it was declared without doubt to the scientific world that the tooth was indeed extremely soft, like cheese. The drifts of dry-red algae, which are invisible to the naked eye but spread throughout the universe, are carried on waves created by planetary magnetic fields, gas tunnels, warp finders, black holes and comet tails.

Pcaethon are normally the size of an average cruise liner and probably weigh about as much as well. Rarely seen because of their low numbers and natural timidity, they are, despite their size, overlooked. It is a situation with which they are quite content.

What Jonah did not know was that a sudden rich wave of dry-red algae had been created by the disappearing Levantine comet's tail, which promised a host of fresh nutrients and reviving particles to any hungry Pcaethon that might be circling the biggest of the asteroids in the belt. The desire to reach every last bit of algae had spurred the lone creature out from its normal area of comfort and away from the belt, following the scent upwards to gulp big pleasurable mouthfuls. As with any field of rich pickings, there was always the possibility of ingesting other not quite so delightful things: ice rocks, ship waste, exhaust fumes and, under certain circumstances, emergency escape capsules.

From within the depths of this great creature Jonah curled himself up even more tightly inside the already tightly crammed capsule, and called to God, who alone could meet him there.

Without question, he had attempted to run – run as far as he could from God, on the loneliest ship, to the loneliest, most insignificant outpost, where no one would be bothered to chase after him. Why would they chase after him? Why would they want him? What role could he possibly fulfil? Surely there was somebody better, somebody less old, less cynical, less retired?

If he had stopped to think about it, even in his running, Jonah would have known that running from God was impossible. It stood to reason that, for the one who had brought everything into being, nothing would be a stretch too far.

So perhaps the logic followed that because he, Jonah, had attempted the impossible (and he had had a pretty good try at it), perhaps God knew he had a knack for it, and that was why God had asked him to do what he had asked him to do.

Jonah had spent too many years talking to himself; perhaps, for a prophet, that was not quite hitting the mark. He talked to himself because it felt safe, and usually a unanimous decision could be reached, to the liking of all involved – but had he, as he now thought, missed the mark and done all his propheting, all the stuff about speaking the word of God, on his own terms? A comfortable prophet, a semi-retired prophet, a prophet on his own terms – was that who he was?

So when he heard the voice calling him, right there in the depths of the Pcaethon fish, he knew that God was there. It wasn't the same as the automatic voice telling him where to stow his luggage or what level to go to, as it had been on the *Sheol II*. This was other, completely other than anything a person could create.

God had put him there in the fish and God had found him there in the fish.

Jonah called to God:

You have thrown me here, in the very heart of nothing.
All your waves and currents have swept me over
and I am banished from you,
and yet you are here with me, I do not understand.
But I will look to you again, to where you are;
as you have chased after me, so must I chase after you.
You long to be found.
I am wrapped about by destruction, barred for ever from life.
Down, down to the very end I have fallen,
but you bring me up.
O Lord, my God, I will remember you.
I will pray to you. I will cling to you.
I will sacrifice to you. I will vow to you.
I will make good.
Salvation comes from God.

All along, it had not been about God forcing him to do what God wanted; it had been about Jonah standing up, answering his God and making a choice. But the only choice he had made was to turn away without answering the call one way or the other before God, and then to imagine that that was a satisfactory answer.

The Pcaethon had eaten too much. Drifts of algae, it thought to itself – typical, they were just like cruise ships. You wait for ages – nothing – and then three come along all at once.

So it was that the fish felt a bit full. It had spent so long enjoying the algae, which it seemed to have had all to itself, that it had lost its bearings. A couple of days went by before it located the asteroid belt again. That feeling of nervous insecurity, away from its cover of floating dry rocks, had probably also added to the uncomfortable gaseous sensation along the enormous length of its alimentary tract. It longed for the sight of a huge, orbiting, porous, pitted stone, then all would be right with space.

The Pcaethon found the end of the belt and swam in among its familiar crowd of asteroids; they welcomed it back with pleasure, as only great big rocks can, and it was at home again. Nevertheless, the growing discomfort in its belly became a painful nuisance and it vowed to itself never to leave the safety of the asteroids again.

Swinging past a satellite planet on the far side of the slightly larger planet where the port of Joppa was situated, the fish had an urgent need to vomit. Vomiting was not polite but had to be done, and afterwards the Pcaethon hid with shame inside a very large hole at the back of the very last rock and let the belt carry it onwards while it recovered.

Jonah and the capsule were not digested; they were instead deposited, inside a great globule of mucus (though in quite a gentle fashion and still very much alive), on to the soft sands of the satellite planet of Kittim. It was a rather dry, unexciting place, but if it was good enough for fish vomit, it was good enough for him. He clambered out of the capsule, once he had figured out the unlocking mechanism, and staggered into hot, dusty, blindingly bright sunshine.

Lower Kittim, Kittim

It seemed to Jonah son of Amittai that God delights in doing the impossible.

The capsule was, he found, disgustingly sticky and slimy as he opened the lid and climbed out. In the great hurry to leave the ship, he had had no time to fetch any of his belongings. The holiday items packed in his backsack – the crystal imaging device, the scroll readers, the snorkel – were now utterly redundant, although, thankfully, his ID papers were still safely crammed inside his robes. So all he had were the robes he stood up in and, of course, his hat with the earflaps and the transmitting skullcap and the ship's overalls underneath his robes. These layers were far too many for such an arid place.

He considered things for a moment. The skullcap would, he imagined, be next to useless now, and it had never fitted properly anyway. The overalls were just not his style at all: someone might mistake him for an itinerant labourer, and he'd had enough of that for a while. Robes were the thing and, of course, his own hat. He was a prophet, apparently not quite semi-retired after all, so he would look like a prophet, so that even if he felt like giving up again, people who saw him would hopefully notice and remind him.

It was a shame to waste the capsule; apart from the fish vomit it seemed pretty much intact, but what on any planet could he do with it? If he'd been nifty with a spanner he could have remodelled it into some form of ground transportation. Instead he undressed out of the overalls and robes and hats and put the unwanted clothing neatly inside the capsule, just in case the ship might wonder where it was and come looking for it. As he was packing the items inside, he found a small undiscovered storage compartment that would have been hidden behind him when he was in the capsule. It contained a bottle of water and some good old ship's biscuits.

'What a find!' he said to himself, and then he stopped and thought.

He had talked to himself, a lot, but then he had talked to God. That didn't have to stop just because he was out of the capsule and back on dry land. God did indeed delight in doing the impossible: Jonah had been thrown off the ship to certain death, but it hadn't happened; he had been swallowed by a creature that shouldn't have been there and he had been spat back out on to this small planet, which was also something that should never have happened, and all that time he had not been alone.

He looked to the heavens – not that God was there particularly, but it was a prophet's habit – and he thanked his God, '... for the storm, because I would have run myself into the ground otherwise; for the captain who stuffed me into the capsule; for the creature that swallowed me and the same for spitting me out; and for the water and the biscuits and the sunshine and ...' After struggling through a few metres of sand, he set out on a road that was bound to lead somewhere, listing all the things that he was truly thankful for.

Jonah watched a transporter cross the sky above him. He couldn't really tell what sort of ship it was – it was too far away – but it did make him wonder about the *Sheol II*. He remembered the moment when the capsule had left the ship and the surprising, albeit brief, silence among the stars. The capsule was not soundproof – that he knew for sure because of all the noises he had heard from outside, while in the fish – so if the ice storm had still been raging he would have heard it. So was that another impossible thing that had happened? The moment he was off the ship, had she been safe again? He believed so.

The captain was not someone who believed in any god, from what he could tell, and yet she had dragged him up from the cabin where he had been sleeping and called on him to pray. 'I was the one who should have been calling people to pray,' he thought, 'but I was the one running away instead.' What Jonah hadn't in fact understood (how could he, given that the capsule had left the ship and therefore left the scene?) was that with his ejection and the resultant abating of the storm, the crew – every man, woman and otherwise – had fallen on their knees in thankfulness to a God they had never known before, a God who with simple readiness could change the course of a comet, yet was also prepared to chase the planets through and through, after the heart of just one person.

Up ahead, fractured in the heat rising from the road, he could see a few buildings. It looked like a small settlement, and he could just pick out someone or something coming towards him along the road, moving a bit faster than he was. He stood and watched for a while, his hand shading his eyes from the brightness of the morning. As the someone or something approached, he could see that it was in fact a person, who, like himself only a few days ago when he had left for Joppa, was pedalling furiously on a scooterer, which also looked pretty much like his.

'Morning,' greeted the man on the scooterer as he stopped beside Jonah, who returned the greeting, understanding that the man was glad of the break for the purposes of breath-catching. They waited a moment in silence together, then, as a way of continuing the conversation, Jonah added, 'Nice scooterer.'

'This old thing?' The man stepped down off the foot pedals and looked his vehicle up and down as if it was the first time he had really had a proper good look at it. 'Yeah, well, it's not done me too badly.' They examined it together in silence, murmuring and nodding their general approval of scooterers.

'You not from round here, then?' the man asked. Then, thinking for a moment, he looked along the road into the distance in the direction from which Jonah seemed to have come, 'You haven't walked, have you? From the city?'

Realising that his recent adventures would be far too much to explain for the purposes of small talk, Jonah hesitated before answering, 'Well … no, actually, I … well, I got a lift.' He pointed back down the road. 'Just got dropped off back there …'

'Ah, I see,' the man nodded, satisfied by a normal sort of answer. 'Well then, I'm off into town. Have a nice day.' Just as he was aligning his feet with his pedals once more, in readiness to leave, Jonah asked, 'Are there any transporters or … anything … from there?' He nodded and pointed in the direction of the settlement, the direction from which the man seemed to have come.

The man turned round to look, as if it would help him answer the question to stare back at the distorted buildings. 'Hmmm, well, you can get a transporter that'll take you back into the city, but if you've just come from there, well you won't want to go back, now, will you?' he laughed. 'So your best bet would be … well, do you want to go off planet? Cos if you do, then the best thing to do would be to go and ask at the postal base for Jim. He does all sorts of trips, does Jim. Yeah, that's most likely your best bet.'

He wobbled off on his scooterer and shouted back over his shoulder, 'He ain't too pricey, either!'

Jonah shouted his thanks in return and carried on his way.

He realised that although he had asked the local man about transport, he hadn't actually thought about what or where he was going to go. He wasn't sure if the original request still stood; if he was honest, he didn't really want to think about it.

The awkward question that he was dreading asking anyone, because one awkward question could only lead to further awkward questions in return, was about exactly where in space he was. He could make a reasonable guess that he wasn't a million light years from home, but he had lost track of everything since he had first boarded the ship.

To his enormous relief, the sign above the postal base read 'Lower Kittim Village Postal Service, Kittim'. He knew where that was, and it meant he wasn't too far from home, after all; he had stood in his back yard and watched the glowing golden rim of the neighbouring planet of Kittim hanging in the sky on many a clear evening. The postal base door even had a delightful little bell that rang as he opened it, which lifted his spirits no end. A few people were milling about inside, mostly those who liked to go and collect their post themselves rather than have a post-bot delivery. Some folks still didn't quite trust them (there had been a case a few years back when some rogue bots had formed a syndicate, skimmed off the profits from penalty costs and blown it all on the latest circuit updates and fancy spray paints).

Jonah went up to the counter and removed his hat with the flaps, firstly because it was rather stifling and secondly because the lady behind the counter looked like the sort who might not take kindly to a shoddy attitude when it came to manners.

'Morning, madam,' he began. Her scowl lifted and she smiled in return.

'Good morning, sir, are you just in today, new in town?'

'Well, yes I am,' he confirmed.

'Lovely to see a religious man in these parts. Our prophet has long since gone.' She pulled a face full of disapproval. 'Ran off with the widow at Sour End.'

'Oh, I see, well, oh dear … I suppose …' Jonah thought that perhaps it wasn't so bad to have run off with a widow; better that than the wife of the meat-man or the baked-goods-man or the wax-light-maker-man. But different areas had their own traditions and their own thoughts on what constituted prophet-like behaviour, expecting it of their prophets but rarely of themselves.

'So, how can I help you then, sir?' she smiled, graciousness itself.

He had forgotten for a moment what he did want help with; he held up a finger. 'Ah, I remember. Transport.'

'Yes?' she replied, urging him on.

'Jim. I need to speak to someone called Jim. Yes, that's it.'

Her whole demeanour changed and the scowl returned. She shuffled some papers on the counter and eventually decided she ought to give him an answer.

'I see,' she said. 'Well then.'

Jonah waited and tried his best effort at a winning smile. Her frowned deepened.

'Through the town, at the end of the road, turn right. There's a run-down, shameful, ramshackle place. You'll find him there. And,' she added, wagging a warning finger, 'watch where you're stepping. He sets traps.'

'You've been so kind, madam, how can I ever thank you?' It was a bit over the top but he felt the situation warranted it and the scowl did lift a little.

She managed a brief 'You're welcome' as he turned to leave.

He was almost out of the door when he heard her call, and for a minute the terrible thought that she might have actually thought of some way in which he could thank her crossed his mind.

'Are you, by any chance, Jonah son of Amittai?' She was peering at some post. This time it was an old-fashioned piece of scroll, the type you unrolled, instead of the sort you read on a screen.

Frozen with his hand on the doorframe, ready to step back out into the sunshine once more, Jonah hesitated. The obvious question was: who would send him post here and now, in this middle-of-nowhere backwater? But to Jonah, the answer was just as obvious. He could step outside, ignore it again, run away again, escape and forget he was a prophet again, or turn around and read the message and go.

'Yes, I am. That's me.'

Jim, Jim, good old Jim; he was an odd kind of fellow. A place like Lower Kittim, Kittim was just the place you would find a guy like Jim, but even here, even in a village named Lower something or other, he was still looked down upon.

As warned, Jonah was very careful where he trod, but he needn't have asked for directions, due to the hand-painted sign at the end of the village with an arrow that read: 'Jim's place, this way, take care! There be traps!'

The path looked clear to start with, but that was when he could see where the path was. It was a path that disappeared, then reappeared in exactly the place where you thought it wouldn't. He took his time. He was not in a hurry. There was a lot to think about.

As he found his way bit by bit, the path led him down, down behind the last few buildings at the end of the village, into not much of anything. Then the way opened out before him into what seemed to be an old quarry site and he spotted piles of scrap metal, plastic, wheels, trolleys, scooterers, containers, derelict transporters and machinery of all kinds. There was a noise, some sort of mechanical whirring or grinding or sawing – being not a technically minded man, Jonah had no idea which. He followed the noise and saw the sparks and waited for, he presumed, Jim to finish. Jim was two of them; or, to put it another way, two of them were Jim.

Jim stopped what he was doing, lifted his goggles, both pairs, took out a scrap of cloth, one from each pocket, and wiped his brows.

'Morning, morning.' With his two voices speaking together, almost at once, he produced rather a pleasant sort of echo.

'Well, good morning. Jim, I presume?' Jonah asked.

'Yes, that's me,' answered Jim, both grinning in a much more friendly way than the lady behind the postal desk. 'How can I help you?'

Jonah thought that, just to be friendly and break the ice, he might ask an interesting question about what Jim had just been doing, but he couldn't think of one apart from 'What are you doing?' and that might lead to the opening of a whole can of engineering worms, in which he would be hopelessly lost. So he thought it best to be direct.

'Well, I wondered if you could give me a lift somewhere; that is, perhaps I can book a trip, if you do trips, or maybe you could tell me how I could get … somewhere?'

Jim studied both his scraps of cloth for a while, a little puzzled, both thinking that this was rather a vague request, and so he thought he would be more direct.

'You want me to take you somewhere?' He spoke deliberately and slowly, as he wasn't quite sure how much this strange prophet man understood.

'Well, yes. Please. That is, if you can, I mean, if it's no trouble. Do you do trips at all?'

Jim wondered if perhaps this old prophet had got a bit lost and had a bit too much sun. He obviously needed to be taken somewhere, but Jim thought he was not sure he wanted the responsibility.

Jonah thought for a moment. 'I can pay … if it would help.'

Jim both laughed. 'You're right there. I wouldn't be doing it for free, me old mate.'

So, then, they seemed to have some sort of agreement; Jonah felt relieved.

'Park yourself over there.' Jim pointed with two right arms, towards a bench which was perched on the back end of an ancient transporter, full of space rust and sun-worm holes.

There wasn't much shade on the bench but it had taken him so long to clamber up there that Jonah thought he had better stay put. He pulled his hat flaps down over his ears against the sunlight and hoped there were no more sun-worms left inside the ancient transporter, which might have a desire to crawl up his robes and start burrowing into an old prophet, mistaking him for just another discarded pile of junk.

He watched Jim as he wandered about his yard, in no particular hurry, sorting things out and putting things away and generally pottering. Instead of getting in each other's way, as one might imagine when there are two of you instead of one of you, they worked seamlessly together as if they had been joined since birth, which of course they had. Both Jims looked up at him. 'So then, where exactly are you wanting to go?'

This was it. This was the crunch. This was make or break. Jonah screwed his eyes up tightly, his hands gripping his knees as if in that very moment he was taking off into space, and answered, 'Nineveh, please.'

His eyes still shut, all he could hear was the beginnings of a deep-throated chuckle, which bellowed up into full-blown raucous laughter, echoing from both Jim and Jim and bouncing off the quarry-stone walls.

When the Jims had finally both caught their breath again and their laughter had trickled away like the shaken-out drops from an empty water bottle, he apologised for his reaction and tried not to break out into laughter once more as he explained, 'Never heard such a funny thing in all my born days. Nineveh …' He stifled a snigger. 'Never thought I'd be asked to take a prophet there! That's marvellous, that is. A prophet to Nineveh … Wait till I tell them down the drinks house … Best laugh I've had all week.'

Jonah wanted to point out that it was *either* 'in all my born days' *or* just 'this week' that his request had been the funniest thing that Jim had ever heard. He was feeling a bit annoyed and, if he thought about it, embarrassed.

That was why he had said 'No' in the first place: he was well aware that he looked far too tame and innocuous; he was sure he was totally the wrong person, the last person in the universe even, to go there and tell them what God had told him to tell them. And there was also that other tiny, niggling thought, like a cocooned larva, that threatened to burst upon the scene – a thought which was laden with the very forgiving, merciful nature of the God he knew. But there it was. That was the point that changed everything. God had told him, and if God had told him (bearing in mind that this was the God who had chased him down the wind and caught him up inside a fish in the whole vast nothing of space and got him out again), there was nothing more to be said.

'Well then,' Jonah began as he made his way carefully down from the bench, 'can you take me, please?'

They agreed on a price and shook hands, twice, and preparations were made. From Jonah's viewpoint, that didn't mean very much at all. Jim showed him where his own transporter was, hidden under a cobbled-together set of tarpaulins and old coats. Jonah expected the vehicle itself to look the same, patched-together, rough-and-ready, but Jim clearly took pride in his machines like nothing else, and this well-loved customised craft sparkled as he pulled back the coverings to reveal its shining, colourful bodywork. You couldn't say it was the latest model, exactly. It had perhaps once been an original one of its type, and it certainly had character, with blow pipes, exhausts, coils, pistons, thermal shielding devices, magnetic gravity insulators ... the list went on and on (of course, Jonah did not really know what half of it was, despite Jim's thorough but useless attempts to enlighten him).

Jonah decided to wait inside the transporter, as Jim said it wouldn't take him very long to get everything ready; it was cooler inside and he made himself comfortable. There was a screen with a whole variety of space maps and charts, and Jonah busied himself with trying to work out exactly where they were and how they would be getting to where they needed to be.

Jim had explained that there would be two drop-stops for refuelling purposes – firstly in Arvad, a stop-off on a small planet marking the halfway point, and secondly in Mari (where Jim would leave him), a mountain town situated on the seventh moon that circled Nineveh itself. Jonah had never been to either of these places, let alone Nineveh, and wondered what it must be like to have no fear of going anywhere, whenever you wanted, like Jim. Or perhaps Jim only went to places when unexpected strangers came wandering by, asking for lifts?

The journey would take a day, maybe two, and it was understood that as well as paying for the fuel and Jim's services as pilot, Jonah would be buying lunch, dinner, supper and breakfast, all breaks included. So in actual fact there wasn't a lot to pack.

They were ready at last. Jonah strapped himself in, as directed by Jim, who both sat in the front seats, as he would naturally be piloting the small ship; and within a whisker, a flash of dust and sun, they were through the wispy atmosphere of Kittim and up into the dark expanse of space once more.

'We won't be meeting any comets, will we, at all?' questioned Jonah, a little bit nervous that he would have to go through all that again, as though colliding with a comet might turn out to be a prerequisite to space travel in general.

'Don't get me laughing again,' laughed Jim, all four hands on the navigation controls and the pilot wheel. 'We don't get anything like that round here. You've been watching too many of them space adventure picture shows.'

Although he had already tried to describe his most recent adventures in space, to which Jim, in rolls of hilarity, had called him an unhinged buffoon, Jonah thought it best not to try and elucidate any further.

'No, no, we just have a nice little trip planned. No problems, nothing to get you upset or frighten you, nothing nasty … well, not until we actually get there, to Nineveh, that is. That's not a place I want to hang around in! It'll be all plain sailing till then, don't you worry. With what you're paying me, I'll be kept going in parts for the next half year or so, and you'll get to Nineveh. So it's lovely and fine all round.'

Thankfully Jim had not asked and did not at any point in the whole trip ask Jonah why he wanted to go to Nineveh. Jonah was extremely grateful about that. He would probably have hovered around the word 'Well …' for a very long time if he had.

'Go at once to Nineveh, that great city, and cry out against it; for their wickedness has come up before me.'

Part Two

From Without

I never thought about it being so cold out here. It was so humid down in the city, and dark, so really red and dark. What is this weather all about? It's unbearable! And another thing that is quite, quite unbearable, to the point of frustration, is why everything has happened that shouldn't have happened, so that now nothing will happen that should happen! Everything is as it was. Nothing has changed except my circumstances and I'm not too impressed about those! It makes me look stupid! I did my bit, I said my piece, I fulfilled my allotted task and what for?

When I think about all I've been through to get this far, I could be properly angry. I know what you are like, God, and this is exactly the reason I ran away – because I knew, I just knew, it would not turn out as I imagined or like you said it would. I might as well have stayed in my semi-retired state or, better still, blown it all and gone the whole hog and thrown in my robes. I just cannot believe this has NOT happened!

Mari of the Seventh Moon

The eatery where Jonah was now having his last meal of the trip, together with Jim, was far and away a different place from the hovering restaurant in Joppa where he had eaten the first meal of his other trip, unexpectedly with Mr Swillows, Underkeeper of the LEGs. They had, of course, eaten in Arvad, which, though nothing to write home about, had at least been civilised, clean and comfortable.

Mari boasted just the one place where a traveller might grab a bite to eat – a café just beneath the landing area – and it was not altogether pleasant. It shook, the whole building shuddering every time a transporter landed or took off from its roof-top flight zone. Jonah envied Jim's four hands, as he could much more easily grab hold of the bowls and cups they were eating and drinking from, to stop them crashing from the slimy table tops to the floor each time the café shuddered.

Splashed across the ceiling above their heads was a hoard of management notices about general bad behaviour and the intolerance thereof. They swam across the ceiling, moving around in rotation so that no one could claim the luxury of ignorance: Do Not Spit! Do Not Smoke! Do Not Brawl! Do Not Throw Food Or Drink! Do Not Slap The Staff! Do Not Put Your Boots On The Bar! Do Not Feed Your Animals Here! Do Not Feed Your Infants Here! (Jonah could not imagine anyone who would actually choose to bring their offspring into a place like this) and finally, Do Not Break Anything!

Each imperative had a carefully worded consequence or fine written in small print at the end. The particular sentence for any breakages was to be landed with the bill for everyone in the café at the time. Jonah wondered how this might benefit the establishment, as it sounded as if it would only benefit the other customers, until he read the next notice that halted above their table: Do Not Leave Without Paying! He concluded that most of these rules were certainly there to be broken and that the management were very grateful when anybody really did pay their bill. He and Jim were decent citizens and had no quibbles about paying their own bill, but to let the plates and bowls crash to the floor in abandon each time there was a landing or take-off, and merrily pay for the disgusting habits of the others, was a line they were not prepared to cross.

To say that they had struck up a deep and lasting friendship since their short journey began would be, at best, an exaggeration. Jim had piloted his beloved craft and enjoyed every minute of it – holding forth on the benefits of his advanced space pilot's training and why he didn't think the new flight regulations were worth the screen digits they were coded on, and shouting previously unheard-of obscenities at any other craft that 'cut him up'. Jonah had at first listened politely, then tolerated, then glazed over at the constant drawl, occasionally jumping with alarm at what he presumed to be the unheard-of obscenities. He had pretended to study the map, as if by staring at the space routes and stars hard enough he might be of some use as a navigator, until Jim pointed out that he had it upside down. 'And anyway,' he had added, 'it's one of them old route maps, without the new flight regulations, which are a load of old …' And off he had flown into a whole new realm of disdain for the modernisation of space travel.

Mari was the last stop for Jim and Jonah. The little café was perched quite literally atop a mountain on the seventh moon of Nineveh, and from here they would part company. He could not say that he felt sad at the thought. Jim was a nice enough fellow, of course – reliable, though a tad dull – and certainly when compared to the slovenly rabble that slopped over the bar in the café like twice-melted cheese, but his mind was filled more with the enormity of what lay ahead.

He had, when he thought about it, chosen both adventures; the first one had been a monumental mistake, and the second …? So far it had proved to be, well, rather unexciting. The first adventure he had chosen himself, flying in the face of all his previous propheting knowledge; the second had been chosen by him, as well as for him. Could it be that it would all be plain sailing from here on in? He looked around the café at the derelict décor, furniture and customers (himself and Jim not included). He looked out of the windows at the busy space traffic pouring in and out of Nineveh and its great red cloak of choking industrial atmosphere, which blurred the distinctiveness of any planetary beauty or formation. In his opinion it did not look promising; it looked as if his sailing down into Nineveh would be anything but plain.

'Payment received in full, thank you very much, Mr Jonah,' announced Jim in a whisper, after they had covertly completed their contract, so as not to attract too much attention. 'Shall we shake hands?' He held out his best two and shook Jonah's with gusto. 'Nice doing business with you.'

Jonah agreed that the business had certainly been 'nice' but said very little in return as his concern was now mostly about himself. Jim was about to fly off this wretched hole of a moon, in the right direction, away from Nineveh. He, Jonah, was about to fly off this wretched hole of a moon, in the wrong direction, towards Nineveh.

Obviously, it all depended on your point of view, and at this precise moment Jonah's point of view told him that to go willingly and with lusty joy down into Nineveh and tell everyone there that they'd got it all wrong was nothing but mad, crazy and suicidal! And anyway, why on any planet would God be interested in them? They just weren't worth it, surely. As these thoughts raced through Jonah's head, he realised just how very human he was and what a poor prophet. Perhaps he should have emphasised his semi-retired state and stayed at home. Perhaps, after all these years of calling himself a prophet, he had been completely mistaken. Perhaps God had asked the wrong person.

Jonah son of Amittai watched as Jim – good old four-handed Jim – gave a vague salute and climbed back up into his glistening craft, which had remained untouched in the holding bay while they had eaten in the café, mainly due to the fact that Jim had paid the extra protection whack preventing any thievery or scratches along the hull. Jonah watched as, with a stylish swerve, Jim took off and headed back home to Kittim. He stood for several moments in serious thought. It was difficult to say exactly what those serious thoughts consisted of; it was just that a general mood of seriousness seemed the only sensible option for his thoughts. Having thoughts before, when he had been trying to escape, had not been a good idea; now, however, he could only think, and think seriously.

The transporter that would be leaving for Nineveh within the hour was filling up, and a right vagabond lot the passengers looked. Jonah then caught a glimpse of himself, a reflection in a patch of polished metal along the underside of the large vehicle beside which he was now waiting; he looked as if he belonged with the vagabond lot. He'd not seen decent washing or grooming facilities for what seemed like an age. With only the robes he stood up in, dusty and still stained by a few streaks of fish vomit; with spiky singed eyebrows and grubby earflaps, and oil under his fingernails, and cracked red cheeks, and no backsack (the presence of which might have made him look a bit less like a pointless drifter), any hope that he could retain any control over his situation finally faded.

'But,' he told himself. 'But … there is always a but …'

Brushing down his robes, giving his hat a solid shake and licking his fingers to flatten his eyebrows, he pulled himself straight and joined the queue.

There were, in fact, two queues, a fact that he had come to realise too late. They were both for the transporter down to Nineveh; they both got you on board ship; but one was for those who already had their names on 'The List' and one was for everybody else who didn't know anything about any List.

'Your name ain't on The List.' So Jonah was informed by a creature far bigger than himself, who probably could have eaten him as a snack if it hadn't happened to be just after lunch time.

Jonah tried his best smile. 'Well … I'm so sorry, but what List is that?'

'You trying to be funny?' The gruff, knobbly, scurfy individual bent down, blowing boiled turnip breath in his face.

'Oh no, of course not. I would never try … never funny, oh no, absolutely not, no, no.' Jonah wondered if his protestations were too much, but it was quite true: he had never been, to the best of his knowledge, funny.

'I was just …' he stammered. 'That is to say, I was just trying to get … I would just like … How much?'

'It says you're not on The List, so it's double.'

Jonah opened his mouth to speak but a sensible thought stopped him just in time, as the words on the tip of his tongue would have probably given him a barrel load of trouble if he had actually uttered them. He was about to say without a care in the world, 'Oh well, that's not a problem. I can pay my way. I have a good semi-retirement fund all set up. Money is not an issue, etc etc.'

Although not given to much subterfuge, Jonah suddenly thought that in this situation it might be quite prudent. He took a look at the crowd around him, the increasingly unsettled queue behind him and the suspicious rabble in the other queue who did have their names on The List. He might quickly become a person of interest if he announced to all and sundry that he had money. Thinking quickly, as well as seriously, he fell into a role that better matched his appearance.

'Double?' he cried aghast. 'I am only a poor old prophet. I can't afford double!'

'Double it is, if you're not on The List.'

'What happens if … I don't, or I mean, I can't pay double?' he managed to stammer. 'Does it mean I can't get on board?' Jonah coughed as if suddenly afflicted with a nasty case of space flu.

The creature in front of him laughed, which was a messy affair, strings of spit and globules of food flying freely. 'Oh, you get on board all right, but who says if you get off again at the other end, eh?'

He leaned in close to Jonah once more. 'You pay me double and I'll see you gets to Nineveh in one piece. Then in future, you're on The List. Get it?'

Jonah nodded in firm agreement and held up his thumb to fit against the screen in the column that indicated double payment. With a heavy sigh and a parting remark along the lines of 'I'm not sure if I will ever eat again …' just to add emphasis, he stepped up into the transporter and sat down in the nearest empty seat he could find.

'Well, I suppose this is what Nineveh is all about. Corruption at the edges and down to the core,' he said to himself. Thankfully the person sitting next to him (difficult to say who or what they were) was snoring already and the ship hadn't even taken off yet, so they would not have been interested in or, worse, taken offence at his conversation starter. There was a strong smell of decomposed potatoes, which was more than likely the cause of his neighbour's intoxicated slumber. It was not going to be easy down there in Nineveh; the thought suddenly struck him that despite having paid double the price, he might not even survive the journey. The thought of being at the mercy of an ice storm in a comet's tail or being digested by a giant asteroid fish did make him think, however, that if he could be rescued from all that, surely it would not be for a far more desolate, mediocre fate in the cesspit that was Nineveh. Jonah son of Amittai closed his eyes and thought about home and wondered if his bean plants would sprout on their own.

There was some sort of explosion and Jonah woke up. He couldn't see anything; it was all pitch black. Then he pulled his hat up from where it had fallen over his face and realised that it wasn't pitch black; it was just a bit dark, a reddish kind of darkness that made you feel as if you were in some great dramatic painting. The passenger next to him was still snoring, although now, instead of leaning away from Jonah against the window, he had altered his angle and was peacefully dribbling across the sleeve of Jonah's robe. The explosion did not appear to have bothered him.

Jonah, now completely free from the visual restrictions of his hat, freed himself from the physical restrictions of his dozing neighbour and managed to stand up from his seat and take in what was going on around him. Were they under some sort of attack? Had war broken out in Nineveh and no one had told him?

'Get your stupid head down!' yelled a voice behind him. 'We're under some sort of attack!'

Another explosion hit, this time very close to the transporter, which rattled like a tin of dried beans. Jonah saw that the other passengers were down on the floor, crawling towards the back of the vehicle.

'This way ...' a voice whispered, very loudly – so perhaps it was more of a shout than a whisper, Jonah did not have time to decide. He just followed the group, all shuffling along like foraging waste beetles.

There was an emergency exit at the back of the transporter: 'Only For Use In Emergencies' it read.

'Well I should think this qualifies …' said Jonah to himself as the exit flew open then ricocheted back on itself. It knocked out the first poor soul in line to escape, who was unceremoniously thrust to one side to make way for all the other, still conscious and capable passengers. Breathless, most of them managed to escape the transporter in time before a third explosion hit, sending the front of the ship up into the space from which it had just come, leaving the back end smouldering on the landing zone in front of them. The other passengers seemed to know what to do in this situation, as if it was an everyday occurrence, and they dragged the gaping Jonah away with them into the shadows of the surrounding buildings.

'You OK?' asked the passenger who had both called out to him in the transporter and then, with others, guided him to relative safety.

Jonah brushed himself down once more, though this time he had a little more dirt on him than before. 'Well, I think so … No bones broken at least.' He waved his arms around and stamped his feet, then winced, not because of any broken bones but because in all the excitement he had forgotten about his temperamental bad back.

'No, I'm fine, really. So do you know what's happened? Who is at war with whom?'

His fellow passenger smiled, patting him on the back, and said, rather than asked, 'Your first time here, eh?'

'Well yes, actually it is,' Jonah replied. He seemed to be saying that a lot recently. Had he really led such a sheltered life? The thought had not bothered him much until now.

The young man, whom Jonah assumed to be his helpful fellow passenger, continued, 'Then let me enlighten you, old man …'

They skulked through empty side streets in semi-darkness, always hugging the walls and talking in whispers; Jonah did not know what to make of anything but he had the sense to copy his companion and follow his every move.

'What happened back there, with the transporter, well that's pretty much an everyday kind of thing.' This young man was indeed very enlightening. 'There's no war as such, unless you mean the constant pointless gang wars. They've been going on for years. One transport company owns this many travel routes, another this many, and there are always others trying to get in on the action. They're riddled with protection rackets, and territorial battles are, as I say, a daily occurrence. Our firm just lost another bus, that's all.'

Jonah remembered The List and was glad he had kept the knowledge of his comparative wealth under wraps.

Then a thought struck him and he asked, 'I'm sorry but you mentioned just now … "our" firm lost another bus?'

'Ah yeah, family firm. I'm a pilot, so I know when to get out quick. I'm very experienced,' he answered as he dived off into a doorway, pulling Jonah with him.

Jonah was surprised: he thought this pilot only looked about fourteen. He had obviously started very young in the family firm.

Another thing that really surprised Jonah was the quietness that surrounded them. The city appeared to be derelict and deserted; they trod in and out, over endless piles of rubble. He wasn't really sure where exactly they were going, but he did feel at least that he could trust this young man.

In a way it was disappointing. He was supposed to be telling everyone to turn from their wicked and terrible ways, to repent and humble themselves before God, who, as he knew only too well and could very recently testify to, had a much better plan for living than they all did. But if there was nobody here to tell, he could only suppose that something must have gone wrong.

This young man did not seem to be very wicked. In fact, the opposite: he had been very helpful. Jonah thought it time he told him so.

'Well, I must say, you have been very helpful, and before we go any further I want to thank you.'

The young man shrugged his shoulders. 'I dunno. I've got a grandad and you look a bit like him, so …'

Jonah thought that that was rather touching, and smiled. 'So which part of Nineveh are we in at the moment?'

The young man laughed. 'Nineveh? Grandad, we ain't in Nineveh, no way.'

'Oh dear, well that's a bit difficult. I thought that's where we were heading, in the transporter, before?'

'Come on, it's not much further.' They passed through a few more empty buildings, travelling onwards and upwards. Then before them a black archway stood out prominently against a blood-red sky – a promising framework of new horizons. Clutching at the neck of his robes, the young man pulled Jonah up and pointed out across the valley below them. Clouds of red dust and jets of fire, which seemed to reach tremendous heights, shot up from the ominous landscape of a vast city. Buildings were high and rugged like a mountain range, standing out at odd angles, as if piled up without much forethought, about to topple over. Bulbous domes topped with monstrous pinnacles were dotted as far as the eye could see and a cacophony of city noise rose to greet them. The sky above the city was boiling with air traffic, swooping lights and slicing wings dividing the dust. The young man patted Jonah on the back again and laughed.

'That,' he said with triumph, 'is Nineveh.'

Nineveh, the Red City

In the time it took to get to the gates of Nineveh, Jonah found out a thing or two about the place – firstly that it was a very important city.

'It's a very important city, is that,' said the young pilot to Jonah as they stood in the archway, gazing down over the tumbled rubble. 'It's the capital of this very planet, it is, and all the seven moons and the three annexed planets further out. Got a lot of trade contracts and business deals and the like, but nothing goes on 'ere that doesn't get the once over from the government buildings down there.' He pointed a precise finger down towards the city, with a stabbing motion. 'We have a monarchy, and a real king at that. No messing around with him. He knows a thing or two about running a place, and if you're not in, you're out.' This time he sliced a precise finger across his extended neckline to emphasise just how 'out' you would be. 'Not that we ever gets to see him at all, mind you. He stays in his own little hygiene box, he do. Can't stand germs and all that sort of thing so he don't mix with people.'

Therefore, the second thing Jonah learned, although he was pretty sure he had heard as much already, was that there was a king and not just a puppet-king, a proper one, though not one you wanted to get on the wrong side of. He discovered that the putting up with of fools was not something with which he amused himself. Watching fools suffer, however, was something in which this king took a great, glinting pleasure, even if it was from behind a sterilised screen.

The third thing he learned about Nineveh was that it was not very straightforward to get into or out of. The young man had taken him as far as he was prepared to go, and although he pointed out which direction to head in next, he would only shake his head and laugh if Jonah asked him to accompany him further.

'This is as far I go, old man. I don't need any more trouble with the likes of that lot down there; I got enough on me own doorstep.' He slapped Jonah on the back in a friendly you're-a-nice-guy-but-not-that-nice sort of way and left him with a rather grubby one-way ticket into the city, an odd-smelling sandwich and a bottle of beer, which made Jonah feel that deep down he was actually quite a concerned, caring sort of chap.

The ticket would get him from the station (the young man had indicated its dimly lit roof, which was hidden among the grim grey hulks that littered the hillside, halfway down the derelict slope towards the city), up to and, with any luck, into Nineveh itself. Feeling a little more informed but no more comfortable about what lay ahead, Jonah son of Amittai lifted the edge of his robes, settled his hat back upon his head, waved a brief farewell to this most helpful of companions and tentatively began his descent to the station.

It was not a totally deserted station; there were a few waifs and strays like him, either loitering or wandering past the dirty, cracked windows of the station building. It could have been any hour of the day or night, as the two large clocks that stood at either end of the platform were both reading different times and with only the occasional digit changing. Jonah had lost complete track of time. He knew it had been after lunch time (or what they had decided on as lunch time) when he and Jim had parted company on Mari, but since then he had narrowly avoided a lynching or mugging or similar when boarding the transporter; he had been dribbled on by who-knew-what; he had slept for one or two hours, possibly more; he had escaped an explosion and been smuggled through a dilapidated, burned-out suburb that was to all intents and purposes a war zone. However, he told himself, he had to remember that he had been given a friendly slap, some decent information, a cheap-rate ticket and something to keep him going, so it wasn't as bad as it could be. He hadn't been swallowed by anything yet.

The ticket was still sticky in his hand, clenched tightly between his finger and thumb. He looked down at it and realised how much optimism he was clinging on to. The greater part of him was yelling to get as far away as possible from everything that was Nineveh, but a little voice of resolution, even though it was gentle and quiet, could still be heard above the din. Safety did not lie in his own wisdom; he felt he had proved that one for sure.

When the helpful young pilot had given him the ticket, he hadn't really questioned it or noticed what was printed on it, but now he came to look at it his heart sank. Not the kind of sinking feeling when you think you're about to be robbed, or you're thrown from the front of the bus to the back of the bus by an exploding grenade, or you realise you've just been swallowed by a space-roaming creature of vast proportions, but more the kind of sinking feeling when you know you've got to get somewhere and the ticket you hold in your hand is for, in your opinion, the worst kind of transport ever invented and it's just screeched to a halt with a sickening pace in the station, right before your eyes. A roller.

Jonah nearly shoved the ticket in his mouth, imagining that he could chew hard for a few seconds, then gulp it down, so as to have no reason whatsoever to get on. But he didn't, and he knew why he didn't: he had to see this through. This one was his responsibility.

Rollers were an ancient form of land transportation used in areas where … well, where nobody really wanted to travel. They were still running because they were almost forgotten about and they required hardly any manpower. They were customer-operated, so you could get on a roller but until you or somebody else hooked up the fat elastic band that would propel the ball-shaped vehicle along the track to the next station, you would just sit there, enjoying the view. Jonah had always thought that was a far better idea – sitting and enjoying the view, that is – than hurtling along a deep, concave, poorly maintained track while spinning out of control. But of course, sitting and enjoying the view didn't get you anywhere, and anyway the view from inside one of these great rolling balls of once-clear resin was not much to write home about, thanks to the grubby residue left by a hundred years of passenger travel.

Several commuters spilled out on to the platform and lay there for a few minutes, groaning until their unwelcome greenish hue dissipated somewhat. Jonah wondered for a moment whether he was the only one boarding the recently disgorged roller for the city; he had no idea of how to operate the band contraption. Together with his little grain of resolution, he was, however, thankful when someone else moved forward, stepping over the recovering bodies in front of the roller, and climbed into the ball.

Jonah settled in, quickly strapped himself into all the belts he could find, and squashed the head restraint down over his ear-flapped hat, smiling as pleasantly as he could at his fellow passenger, who then frowned as it dawned on her that she would have to do the honours and get the vehicle in motion. She was a large woman, not much younger than Jonah himself, so it was not an easy job for her to clamber across to the hole in the ball that was at present behind them and yank the band over the winder while holding the pull-cord tightly until she herself was strapped in and settled. Muttering under her breath about the lack of manners and other terrible vices which were to be found in all foreigners, she then asked him, 'You going to the city?'

'Well, yes. I am, actually,' Jonah replied, happy that at least she didn't appear to be too put out by operating the mechanism.

'Good,' smiled the woman, 'because there is one more stop before we get there and YOU can be a gentleman and operate the next one!' She smiled back at him with undisguised triumph and let go the pull-cord.

Jonah wanted to explain to her that he was a semi-retired prophet and not a gentleman, but it was too late for that and he screwed up his eyes as the ball sprang forward with the all the attack of a cat stalking its prey. He was extremely glad he had decided against eating that sandwich.

The one good thing about the rollers was the fact that they were fast. It was an awful way to travel, however; nothing but light speed could top it, at least over short distances, and they were at the next station within a few minutes.

Unfortunately for Jonah, he found himself suspended upside down as the ball came to rest, so unstrapping himself was looking hazardous, especially as his fellow passenger lay directly beneath him. He thought she might not be so convinced of his presumed gentlemanly status if he were to drop right into her lap unannounced, so he considered it best to say something to that effect.

'Well, we are in a little predicament, aren't we ...?' he simpered.

'It's your turn. I'm not moving.' She folded her arms, at least as far as the restraints permitted, and lifted her chin, looking out through the smeary walls of the roller on to the station platform.

Unfortunately for the woman, though fortunately for Jonah, some new, much younger passengers entered the ball; they seemed very keen on operating the roller. Paying no attention to the existing passengers within the vehicle, the gaggle of scrawny kids scrambled among legs, arms, belts and braces and began to tussle over who would operate the mechanism. After a few hearty slaps round several ear-holes, brawn won and the smaller kids flung themselves back against the sides of the ball, spreadeagled, grabbing hold of whatever they could to steady themselves and whooping with anticipation.

'Isn't that a bit dangerous?' whispered Jonah to the nearest child pressed flat up against his shoulder. The child just laughed and shouted, 'Free-riding! Let's go, Pops!'

The biggest kid, who had hold of the pull-cord and was crouched down ready to pounce as the ball sprang to life, yelled his loudest and let go.

Jonah hardly dared open his eyes as they lurched to a halt at what he hoped was the final station. He heard the kids before he saw them. Someone vomited just to his left and, even though there were a few moans and groans, most of them were still laughing.

'Hooligans!' voiced the woman as she disentangled herself from a child at her feet. After some manoeuvring she was out of the ball and flopped over a nearby pile of newspapers, searching in her large handbag for a comb and some lipstick with which to put all things in order.

'Nice one, Pops,' muttered the child who had vomited as he collapsed down on to the floor of the ball below him.

Although Jonah had some serious concerns about the state of these children, who, if they carried on this dangerous practice, riding without restraints, he feared would suffer some brain injury or, worse, would not live to see sense or adulthood, he felt that no admonition from him would be enough to change their ways. They were obviously roaming the wastelands and perhaps the city without structure, education or positive input, which might otherwise set them on the road to becoming decent citizens. The depth of depravity, disinterest and poverty that had led to such a state was perhaps one sign of the true situation in Nineveh. If he felt his caution would be wasted on these children, then how much more pointless would it be for the city as a whole?

He loosened his straps, toppled forward and melted on legs of jelly on to the solid platform floor, just outside of the roller.

'Move your carcass!' bawled a voice above him. Jonah blinked his eyes open and struggled to a sitting position where he was, in the red dust of the station platform.

'You can't stop 'ere. Move it, Grandad!' This time he was attacked by a large bristled brush, which added value to the demand. Jonah wondered whether it was perhaps just a friendly colloquial term with which he found himself being so frequently addressed or whether, in his increasingly dishevelled state, he had begun to resemble an aged father of fathers.

Tentatively stretching his limbs, he found that he could just about 'move it' and gathered himself and his hat together, apologised to the sweeper, bowed and staggered away. The red dust got everywhere, no matter how much he brushed himself down, and as he began to notice the busy throng of people scurrying back and forth, around the checkpoints at the city gates which now loomed in front of him, he realised that they too moved about amid a dim scarlet haze. He was about to enter Nineveh. He was about to fulfil his task. He was about to become a full-time prophet once more. He was probably about to meet his end and he hadn't even had time for a bath. This was it.

Jonah son of Amittai shuffled up towards the vast, monumental, crumbling, god-forsaken gateway, which hung in the red dust as if descended from the dark clouds above. His neck strained high as he took in the enormity of it all and stepped on up to join the crowd.

At least he had a better idea now of what time of day it was, because the local hawkers were keenly pushing their breakfast wares on the people as they passed. The morning news-screens were flickering with pictures of the king and his government spouting forth bland statements of peace, plenty and profusion, of wealth and security, of Nineveh's universal dominance and provision to all its people – to those that held the party line, of course.

He was photographed, front and profile, and was forced to add his grubby thumbprint once more, indicating the spot marked 'pleasure' when asked the purpose of his visit. It was nowhere near accurate but it was the simplest way of completing the form and would allow him easy entry for up to a week. There was never a box for 'propheting'.

Despite the touch of scrutiny on entry to the city, the process was quite anonymous and Jonah could not have felt more insignificant. In a way, that was good: he was never comfortable with too much attention. However, he realised that his commission would require significance and he had no idea how you got hold of it. Through the gates he walked, trying not to notice the decapitated corpses hanging from the posts which lined the main high street in front of him. He could only imagine what terrible crimes they must have committed to be so punished and so displayed, but then he thought that he did not really have such a bright imagination after all and it was best not to try and imagine these things.

Packs of foul-mouthed slave traders driving their neck-chained wares along the main street; dull-eyed children under orders to beg in the dust; blatantly marauding vigilantes stomping in the gutter: these were the most instantly obvious indicators of a city steeped in evil, and Jonah could only push forward as he tried to come to terms with it and ignore it, at one and the same time. There was no escaping the fact that the job he had to do was monumental.

What he did think, though, was that a good breakfast might just set him up for the monumental job ahead, so he found an overflowing rubbish pile that was glaciating out from a side alley and carefully deposited the kindly meant but nonetheless dubious sandwich on top, with the idea that he would head on into the city and find somewhere nice to eat. The thought grew that maybe he could find somewhere to have a wash and brush-up, even catch up on some sleep – a hotel with en suite facilities and a glorious bath. The picture was looking more and more appealing; he saw gold taps and a tray of eggs and bacon on toast, and clean white pillows, and …

'Penalty for littering – immediate incarceration or two years' pay. Stand forth and account for yourself.'

Jonah whipped around to find himself face-to-face with a security-bot, which took the form of a loudspeaker, angled downwards at him from atop a hovering city warden vehicle that hung in the air above the street.

'Name yourself. Account for yourself.'

Sadly all thoughts of hot water, bubbles and eggs vanished as he blinked into the screen, wondering why he, of all the nobodies who had left their rubbish on the creeping mound, had been caught red-handed. And then, out of the dusty cloud around him, a marvellous thought presented itself.

'Well, hello.' He coughed and started again. 'Hello. Yes, I am Jonah son of Amittai and I am happy to pay the fine mentioned. But I was just wondering …' He was only asking; what was the worst that could happen? He didn't stop to think about the hanging corpses at the city gates. 'I was wondering if I could possibly borrow your vehicle and your lovely little speaker here?' He patted the screen, as if attempting to win the affections of a newly acquainted pet. 'I am happy to pay for the privilege.'

It was risky, very risky, but in that split-second wait it might just pay off. The loudspeaker crackled as if frantically flicking through its billion layers of code for an appropriate response and found that there wasn't one. The screen died and drooped and the vehicle hovering above descended rather rapidly and landed in a cloud of red gravel and litter as Jonah jumped aside just in time. The vehicle doorflap rose and a tubby security guard heaved himself out, pulling off his gloves and wiping his forehead.

'It ain't half boiling in there. Glad of the break, I am,' he puffed, and stood before Jonah, hands on hips, looking him up and down. So it wasn't really a security-bot after all but just a fat, sweaty guard who was already fed up with his day's work.

'What you want Her for any way?' He jerked a thumb backwards indicating the vehicle. 'Gonna start a revolution, eh?' he laughed, enjoying his joke.

Jonah laughed as politely as he could in return and wanted to answer that he supposed he was sort of trying to start a revolution, but thought better of it.

'Well, actually,' he began, 'I am sort of, well, sort of … selling something, I suppose. And I rather thought that She,' he nodded towards the loudspeaker and the vehicle, 'might just come in handy. Reach a wider audience and all that sort of thing?'

The guard rubbed his chin and muttered something like, 'Hmm, I dunno, hmm.'

'As I said earlier,' Jonah continued, pushing his case, 'I am willing to pay...' He took his hat off so that the guard could see the pleading eyes of an honest prophet. A moment passed as the prophet widened his eyes as far as he could and the guard narrowed his in return as he considered the proposal.

'Double. You pay me double the fine, right?' the guard finally answered. 'So, you pay for your crime and I get the money for the wife's face transplant. Every man's a happy man. Right?' The guard spat in his palm, then stuck out his hand to clinch the deal.

Jonah could not believe he had pulled it off, and in the excitement the thought of fresh hotel sheets and fluffy pillows paled in comparison.

'Now then,' continued the guard after the payments had been made, the instruction manual had been found lurking beneath the driver's seat and he had let Jonah have a little practice on the loudspeaker. 'No funny business. This is my transporter, right? My transporter: my job. Don't try to pick anybody up for littering or anything worse, and don't use the main city lines. Just stick to the back alleyways and get back to this gate by sundown.'

Jonah nodded, eager to show he understood everything (although he wondered, in the dark fog and general dinginess, how easy it would be to tell when the sun went down), and as the guard pulled the door down to shut him in, all of a sudden he was glad of the one-way glass.

'Well, old bean,' he said to himself, 'what have you done?'

He stopped for a moment, held his head in his hands and whispered, 'What have I done?'

He looked up again and saw the lost, moody crowds that filed across the screen in front of him. He was a prophet, he had taken a huge chance and he had a job to do. In fact, he had, when he actually thought about it, really chosen a pretty good method, and he congratulated himself. 'I can remain insignificant. I don't have to look inspiring from inside here. It's the words that are important and now I can make them very meaningful indeed.'

He pressed the ignition button and pushed a bit too hard on the motion lever, sending the transporter wildly up into the red cloud. He was no pilot and not even on a tour of duty with good old Jim had he picked anything up. His squealing cries bellowed out of the loudspeaker and a few people did actually stop in their tracks and look up.

'Very meaningful indeed!' he said to himself.

'Forty more days and Nineveh will be overturned!'

He was getting into this now. He had a bit more of a handle on the controls once he had employed the autopilot system, and the loudspeaker was simple. He didn't change the patter much because he thought the words spoke for themselves, really. He had no idea if he was straying across the main lines that the guard had warned him about or not. He trusted the craft to drive itself; he hoped it didn't matter too much. It was all going rather well and he was pretty sure he had managed to cover a large part of this vast city. People were stopping, people were listening, and yet, so far, no one had stopped him.

The carmine glow of the cloud and dust seemed to be diminishing. Perhaps what the guard had referred to as sundown was approaching; he had to find his way back to the gateway. From a higher vantage point he thought he could see the gateway, or at least *a* gateway, and he managed to turn the transporter and point it in that direction. The impetus to use the loudspeaker had waned and he now really did want that bath. He hoped he had done enough to merit one.

Even from inside the transporter he could tell that outside there was now a strange, pervading silence; he sensed it even before he found out how to open the door of the vehicle to get out. Maybe it really was that late and everyone had gone to bed. But then, he thought, a city like Nineveh never sleeps; even an old prophet like him knew that. He pulled the driving goggles away from his face, revealing a large pair of pale-framed eyes, and took the gloves off, just as the guard had done. He'd been right about the heat inside the driver's cab; Jonah hadn't noticed it till now, but his skin and his insides felt dry and dusty and thirsty. The streets were absolutely quiet and dead, as if a bomb had been dropped, a silent bomb that had only affected the minds of the people and had left the city structure untouched.

He was as amazed as anybody when the very same guard whose transporter he had earlier purloined walked up to Jonah where he stood leaning against it as if he did this every day of his life, and fell on his knees before him, sobbing into the dust. Jonah looked around to see if there was something to explain the situation. Then a few more people came out from the doorways, from inside the shops where they had been waiting, from behind their market stands, from off the city transport lines, which stood as silent as the grave. This was all very unexpected and not at all what was supposed to happen. Not that Jonah had given much thought to what he supposed should happen; he had been intent on fulfilling his duty as quickly and as painlessly as possible, with the hope of soon disappearing back home.

Touching the guard's shoulder, because he didn't know what else to do, they both jumped at the sudden contact. Jonah was not sure what to say.

The guard looked up at him, his ruddy cheeks lined with salty tears.

'I didn't know …' he stammered, 'I didn't know what you were going to say … Tell me, tell me what you said again?'

'What did I say?' Jonah frowned, feeling that he didn't quite understand the question.

The guard pointed up to the clouds. 'When you were up there … Say it again.'

Jonah looked up and then hung his head, wishing he could be once again securely hidden behind the dark screens of the vehicle. It was an awful lot easier when you were hidden in a box and with something else to speak for you.

'Well,' he began, shaking the dust from his old hat for a distraction, 'I said … amongst other things, forty more days and Nineveh will be overturned …'

The guard broke down into sobs again, and all that could be heard were the quiet cries of regret and despair from the others around them, all on their knees.

Jonah did not understand.

He laid the goggles and gloves down in the dust next to the guard and gingerly moved away. It felt as if a huge catastrophe had hit the city and somehow it was his fault. This was one of his darkest moments, when he began to wonder why he had ever become a prophet in the first place. Words had a power that he would never fully comprehend, especially the words that came from God through a prophet – words of judgement, truth and consequence.

Then he noticed that the gentle, painful soul waves that were flooding the streets in response to his words were now added to by a growing hum, as a much larger and obviously more important transporter broke through the clouds above him and a searchlight beam danced around the street until it found him, locking him in its gaze. Another loudspeaker hailed down towards him and he was struck again by the power of such a device.

'Who are you?'

Jonah shielded his eyes from the glare and looked back up towards the voice.

'I am Jonah son of Amittai.'

There was a moment's pause.

'Jonah son of Amittai, the king wishes to hear you speak.'

The King, a Very Important Man

Jonah was vaguely satisfied. At least he got to have a bath. It was not exactly the rich, bubbly, nice-smelling kind of bath that he had earlier imagined, but it was hot and wet and deep, and there were fresh towels of a reasonable thickness, and he had been offered a cup of tea and toast. So all in all it wasn't too bad an outcome so far, after being arrested, as he imagined he must have been.

When he came to think about it, though (and Jonah, like most people, did tend to think, especially when lying in the bath), judging by the nature of the treatment of criminals that he had already observed in Nineveh, giving them a bath and something to eat did not quite seem to fit the pattern. Perhaps they were lulling him into a false sense of security. But would they really bother doing that with someone like him? Perhaps they thought he was an agent of espionage, working undercover, under very deep cover; perhaps, with his shabby prophet robes and his general dishevelment, he appeared so inept as to actually throw suspicion back in his direction. The one thing he was sure of, though, was that he had fulfilled his task, and in the warm comfort of the bath he realised that he had no desire to run away. The water would leave him clean and refreshed and perhaps he could then think about what to do next.

He dried himself and, with a fat towel wrapped around his waist, he went in search of his robes. The bathroom was a large tiled room, quite clean, though old-fashioned in style; the floor was cold under his bare feet as he pattered about, looking for his clothes. He was sure he had left them on one of the chairs or blanket boxes, or under some towels, perhaps. There was a knock at the door. Jonah hesitated for a moment before calling back, 'Come in?'

The door opened and what he presumed to be a servant of some sort entered and placed his newly washed and dried robes on the chair nearest the door, before quickly leaving him alone again in the room.

'Well, I must say …' Jonah went to retrieve his robes, marvelling at the new layer of bright colour which had been discovered underneath all that accumulated dust and dirt, and at how swiftly the whole thing had been achieved. 'And they haven't shrunk, either!' he laughed, so pleased with this little touch of civility.

A dressed and revitalised prophet poked his head out of the bathroom door and peered in both directions along the dark corridor. It had all happened in a moment. He remembered boarding the large transporter that had hailed him by the city gates. He remembered being strapped into a chair with a safety belt as the vehicle had swerved off – in the direction of the king's residence, he presumed. He remembered being asked if he would like anything in particular and he remembered that his immediate reply had been that he wanted a bath. So there he was, bathed and ready for …?

'Well, I suppose I'm ready to see the king,' he said to himself. Stepping out suddenly and silently from the shadows, a servant stood before him and said, 'Please, sir, this way.' He held out an arm to indicate the direction in which they should go and then proceeded to lead the way along the corridor. Jonah shrugged his shoulders and thought that, as he had been asked so politely, the least he could do was to follow.

The corridors and rooms they passed through were not outwardly excessively ostentatious; they were just numerous. Occasionally Jonah glimpsed a view of the city outside from a window or a balcony; it was sullenly dark and unmoving with only a few lights pinpointed across the red cloud.

The servant finally stopped outside a large door, pinned in a code on the small plate beside it and pushed the door open, allowing Jonah to pass through. The door shut behind him with a soft click.

'Are you clean?' asked a voice at his side in the shadows.

Jonah hesitated; he thought that that was a very pertinent question indeed and required some internal debate. He looked up and saw the face of what he presumed to be a royal official who must have been waiting inside. As the answer seemed not to be forthcoming, the official asked the question again, this time with a bit more clarification: 'Are you clean? Have you bathed?'

Now Jonah understood where this was going and replied with warm certainty: 'Oh yes, thank you. A very enjoyable and much-needed experience.'

It seemed a small bow was in order to add emphasis to his truly felt gratitude, so he added one and waited for what would happen next.

'Then you may view his most powerful, most sanitary, most hygienic majesty,' murmured the official with a small nod in return, and a curtain that stood at the far end of the room they were in was pulled aside, revealing a very dark viewing screen. Jonah looked, straining his eyes to make anything out on the screen, wondering whether it would flicker into life or brighten up at all. He made as if to step forward to get a better look, but the official's hand was swift to hold him back.

'It is not permitted to step any closer at this time, not unless his majesty wishes it. He is a very important man.'

'Oh, well then ...' was all Jonah could say in reply, though he was not sure what to do next. It was an uncomfortable moment, but then again, he thought, not anywhere near as uncomfortable as some he had recently been through. Perhaps there would be a fanfare or a procession or something to announce the king's arrival. Perhaps there would be drinks and nibbles; he was feeling rather peckish, despite his earlier meal.

They waited, and then, almost imperceptibly, the screen lightened a little and the shape of a person beyond the screen became clearer. It was a man, and a man of great height – unless, of course, he was standing on a box – but apart from that, any further details of his features or clothing were quite indistinguishable.

'Behold, his most powerful, most sanitary majesty, the king,' whispered the official, who bowed. Jonah quickly followed suit and waited still further. His knees were beginning to ache a little, not to mention his back, and he was extremely relieved when the official slowly raised himself.

The king spoke, his voice hailing them through the screen: 'Is this Jonah son of Amittai?'

With another bow, the official replied that it was, and Jonah felt the need himself to bow yet again. He had done his fair share of royal events and conferences in his time, but this was a foreign culture and it seemed best policy to copy the person next to him and not to make any rash or sudden movements.

'He is a small man,' stated the king.

'Indeed he is, your majesty,' stated the official.

If Jonah had been a hot-headed sort of fellow, he might have taken umbrage at this personal, unacknowledged description. However, he merely frowned and pulled himself up a little.

'Is he clean?' asked the king from behind the screen.

'Yes, your majesty, he is sanitary,' replied the official.

Jonah nearly burst out that he most certainly was, and that that aspect of his person had never been brought into question.

'Then let him come a little closer,' said the king.

The official took Jonah's elbow and they stepped a little closer to the screen, although the king still appeared as vague as before.

'Ah, now I can see him all the better.'

Jonah could only presume that the screen was some sort of one-way affair, as his view of the king was certainly no better.

There were several more minutes of waiting while the king looked Jonah up and down.

'Jonah son of Amittai. I have heard things,' said the king.

'Well, yes, your majesty …' This was not an easy conversation so far, thought Jonah.

'I have heard things about you,' continued the king, his voice giving nothing away.

'Well …' said Jonah, 'indeed … your majesty,' he added after a quick nudge from the official.

'You are a prophet.' This was, he felt, quite an obvious statement.

'Well, yes … your majesty,' Jonah simply acknowledged. He thought it not wise to go into all the details about his supposed semi-retirement, the running away, the *Sheol II*, the comet, the fish, old Jim and the arrival in Nineveh.

'Tell me what you have been saying in this great city of Nineveh, to my people, to my city.'

It was tricky to tell whether or not there was any anger in this demand from the king. Without seeing his face, it was impossible to judge. Jonah thought he ought to tread carefully and tried to think of a way in which he could couch his prophet's task in respectful, majestically acceptable terms. While he was scrambling around in his head, rearranging his thoughts, the king spoke again.

'I want to hear exactly the words that you have spoken to my people. I want to hear it for myself. Do not hold anything back.'

He knew it. He knew that this endeavour could not end pleasantly with a nice hot bath, a plate of toast and a polite chat with the king. Ah well, he thought, this is all part and parcel of a prophet's existence – a real shame, nonetheless.

'Your majesty,' he began, and launched into the very same words he had spoken over the city just a few hours before. At the end he bowed and waited, the sweat pouring off his forehead as he stared at the floor.

'Your most powerful, most sanitary, maj…!' With utter consternation the official cried out at the king's reaction. 'You cannot leave your … It is most unsanitary! Most unhygienic! I beg of you!' he continued, his fingers clawing through his hair in panic. Under his breath, he glanced across at Jonah and muttered, 'What have you done …?'

Jonah looked up and saw that the king had disappeared from behind the screen and at that very moment was rushing out through a door at the side. He was not a tall man, after all; he was, in fact, not much taller than Jonah himself. He must have been standing on a box. It was as if the split-second decision to jump down from whatever it was that had been falsifying his stature was an indication of another, much more significant decision. As a king he had been all too well aware of how his city and planet were run, and he had not been without responsibility. He had been as deeply involved in the greed and cruelty as any one of the traders or officials or ganglords and he couldn't escape the truth that the overwhelming burden of responsibility lay at his feet like a rotting corpse. And so he had stood on a box, he had hidden inside a box; he had sealed himself inside a germ-free tomb in an attempt to rid himself of the stinking burden.

Running up to Jonah, who shuffled back in momentary fear, the king clung to this poor prophet's robes with tears streaming down his face; it was just like the guard all over again.

The official was frantically whispering at Jonah's side as if there was now a sudden and desperate need to fill in the blanks and explain the behaviour of the king.

'His majesty never, and that is an absolute fact, he NEVER leaves his royal quarters, which are sealed and sanitised and totally free from harmful bacteria and disease spores and, and, which have always remained so. I can't bear to think what would happen … what is now going to happen to his majesty … in this atmosphere. He will die … it is so terrible …' A moment's hesitation to catch his breath brought an added realisation: 'And I will die!'

Meanwhile the king was at Jonah's feet, sobbing on the floor like a prisoner bargaining in a last-hope supplication, the remaining shreds of dignity most recently fallen away.

Jonah had no sense of his place within this scene of desperation. His place was somewhere very far away, a million light years away from this sorry planet – a little unassuming hole in the hillside he called home, where he grew vegetables with moderate success and ignored the neighbours, also with moderate success, and where he had presumed his years of quiet semi-retirement would play out.

After some minutes it seemed that the king had recovered himself to some extent (unlike the official, on the other hand, who was cowering in the corner, his jacket pulled up over his head). Jonah took a few steps backwards as the king, rising from the floor, nodded respectfully towards him before hurrying out through the main door, which led out into the corridor and the palace rooms beyond.

The prophet stood and waited, unsure whether to approach the whimpering official or to leave him alone with his thoughts. He chose the latter and wandered out of the door through which the newly released king had just fled, in an attempt to retrace his steps.

There was a commotion, the noise reaching him along the corridor, and Jonah, with little degree of confidence, followed the sound. People carrying papers, documents, clothes, flasks of water, towels, blankets, bottles of medicine and such like were rushing through doors and hallways in strange and hushed tones of fear and panic, much like the official he had left in the royal anteroom. In his wake the king was producing a wave of dignified anxiety, which began to sweep through the royal buildings, turning everything upside down.

Doors flew open before the king as, in the greatest display of majesty ever witnessed, he flung them aside.

For a man who never left his hermetically sealed chamber, he had a pretty good knowledge of the palace layout, and in no time at all he stood in front of the last set of huge doors, which now stood between him and the rest of the city of Nineveh. He was breathing heavily and, for a moment, doubt threatened to topple the bright, sudden tower of understanding he had so very recently constructed. The words of Jonah had had a most powerful and most sanitary effect, majestic in their simplicity and clarity. He was king of Nineveh and, as king, he had failed; the city had fallen to unknown depths and he had locked himself away, sealing himself up tightly from any responsibility while still allowing himself to enjoy all the benefits of the wealth created from the city's depravity, greed, power and ugliness. He had commanded torture, executions and slaughter while remaining utterly removed.

The bulging crowd of royal servants, officials and straggling onlookers, the group to which Jonah himself now belonged, heaved up behind the king, waiting for his next move, clutching their equipment – cleaning sprays, antibacterial ointments, scrubbing brushes, pristine plastic sheeting – items which might possibly aid him through any resultant effect of this totally unforeseen circumstance. His next move could produce any number of unpredictable events, all of which they would be powerless to prevent.

Jonah could see as he peered behind the elbow of somebody carrying a basket of cleaning materials that the king now had his hands on the doors and was about to push them open. A sudden voice from the crowd squeaked a warning before stifling itself in the hushed silence, which threatened to swallow them all. Jonah knew what it was like outside those doors – the red dust, the darkness and squalor, the poverty and pain, the madness and dullness of human existence – and here was the king of all of it, opening the door.

As a blast of red dust blew in, they all shielded their eyes – all except the king, who, with a sudden gasp, drank it in, stumbling down the steps and falling on to his knees on the ground. He lay in the dust, picking up handfuls of it and pouring it over himself like a child on the beach with his first feel of running sand. Then, tearing his kingly garments away, he shed them, embracing the dust as it covered his naïve, trembling figure.

Nobody knew what to do, least of all Jonah. He had expected reactions, that was true enough – anger, maybe, jeering, scepticism, disinterest – but to be listened to so immediately, and for the words he had propheted to be so readily heard and received, as if they were grains of fire powder which had only needed a spark to ignite them, well, that was as far from expected as he was as far from home.

From the dark scarlet corners of the alleys, side streets and buildings which surrounded the large plaza in front of the palace, the people of Nineveh emerged, creatures gingerly tasting the air for the first sign of danger in this wholly new atmosphere pouring over the city. They too had shed their exclusive garments, sensing the urgency of a truth laid bare. In bags, boxes, bits of old curtain and carpet they had wrapped themselves, the ugly cumbersome nature of their coverings a reflection of themselves.

Kneeling in the dust together with their king, whom they hardly recognised, they murmured and wailed in gentle tones, remembering and lamenting the state of their city and their planet and the moons beyond. Previously callous and bloodthirsty, greedy and inhuman, the toughest and coldest of them all were lying in the cardinal dust, whimpering and tortured by lashes of guilt.

The palace officials and staff spilled out along the steps, dropping their feeble equipment, and fell on their knees. They had heard the words – Jonah's words, God's words – but fear for their king had mingled with fear for their lives, and only now, on witnessing this dramatic demonstration, did they allow themselves to be overcome. Jonah alone was left hiding behind the door. He wanted to be small, smaller than he already was; he wanted to be somewhere else; he wanted to leave this city.

For several hours the king and the people of Nineveh remained in the dusty streets rather than going home or resuming work, as if those acts might dispel the revelation. The king, who had been as remote as any king could ever be while still being a king and living inside the city, was now before them in red dusty flesh, and nothing else mattered quite as much any more. As a heavy, dark dawn broke beyond the city gates, he lifted his head and staggered to his feet to acknowledge his gathered citizens.

Looking around for an official, he renewed his royal guise once more and summoned those nearest to aid him. Ever vigilant for the king's requirements, one of them stood and bowed, awaiting his command. There was, all at once, the sense of an age gone by when a king was truly a king, visible among his people, not a resolute prisoner in a tightly sealed box, fearing human contact and blind to the sunken depths of a bereft nation.

Speaking in his official's ear, the king requested a vehicle, and staff hurried off to fulfil the necessary requirements, glad of the brief resumption of normality.

Within minutes, a sleek, glistening cruiser hovered over the roof of the palace and descended into the plaza, dispersing the people and the dust in short bursts as it settled. The king refused all offers of more appropriate royal apparel, choosing instead to climb into the craft half-dressed and glowing with bright dust. A few staff joined him as pilots and crew and, as quickly as it had appeared, the cruiser left the plaza in a repeat of Jonah's previous stunt.

Hailing them all from the loudspeaker device on board, the king spoke, and just as Jonah's words had penetrated every nook and cranny of Nineveh, so now did the king's.

'By decree of the king and his officials: do not let any one of you or your families or your livestock taste anything; do not eat or drink. But cover yourselves, as I have done, in shame, in rags, rubbish and dust. All of us, we must call urgently on this God that we have heard about today. We must all give up our evil ways and all violence. Who knows? God may still relent and with compassion turn from his fierce anger, so that we may be saved from destruction.'

Just as, the day before, Jonah had done, so travelled the king along the vast length and breadth that was the city of Nineveh, relaying his message until the meagre light from the sun had diminished and the day was ended.

As for Jonah son of Amittai, he had waited behind the door, hiding from something he knew nothing about. He was weary and irritated and he realised that he had not slept properly for several days. The people of Nineveh had not slept; nor would they for the immediate future, as their understanding of the words spoken by himself and now the king grew. He had lived through some very strange events in his time, especially in recent days – most especially, however, this day. This hour was the strangest yet. Everything was heavy, it seemed to him, weighted with portent and the burden of momentous change, and he decided that this was his cue to leave. The ugly, distasteful, gaudy, crime-ridden city was doomed whichever way you looked at it, and he did not want to be there when its time was up.

The palace was to the far east of the city, high on a plateau just within the gates, so he knew that leaving the city should not be too difficult or take him too long. He headed back inside the palace and wandered, lonely in a small cloud of dust that diminished with every step. The rooms and hallways were virtually deserted, although sometimes he caught a glimpse of a scurrying footstep here and there as he passed through, searching for a back door, if such a thing existed in a palace. His heart felt sad and small, and his feet felt tired and sore, and he did not know what he was going to do next. There would be no transport out of the city, he was pretty sure of that. Already everything had ground to a standstill and he had no idea what was waiting for him on the far side of the walls – more of the same derelict gangland that he had been escorted through on his first approach to the city, he presumed.

The view through a window in the last room he came to showed him a great courtyard, where dozens of vehicles and mounds of machinery and military equipment stood in readiness for royal command. Lolling guards hung about in seated groups, huddled before a few small fire-pits, heads in hands, as they too had heard the messages and were now bereft of direction and purpose. Straining his eyes, Jonah could see through the darkness what appeared to be part of the city wall at the far end of the courtyard. He wondered if there might possibly be another door or gateway which would take him away from this grief-laden place, so he picked up his pace in the hope of finding a way down to the courtyard.

As he had thought, there were some winding stairs and a narrow door, which eventually opened out beneath an archway in one corner of the courtyard. He decided to try to move along unnoticed, dodging from shadow to shadow, in case the guards were more alert than they appeared; he slipped as niftily as he could between the stationary vehicles and archways and corners until he was further away, far from the palace. He looked back and saw the last glint of fiery sunlight above the parapet and top tower of the palace, where a single solid black flag, edged in scarlet, wavered at half mast in the breeze.

Reaching a small wooden door with a rusty broken padlock, he wrenched it open, pulled his hat down tightly over his ears and stole through to the other side.

From Without

Why has this dreadful weather come? Why right now? Why am I destined to be always on the wrong side of everything all the time? I thought I had had more than my fair portion of calamitous situations; surely I've learnt my lesson, so why are you making me go through yet more discomfort and trouble? I have done what you asked of me and in the process I have suffered not inconsiderably, and yes, I am aware that most of that was of my own making, but why tease me with a taste of reward and then leave me abandoned on this hell-hole of a planet?

O Lord, is this not what I said when I was still at home? I knew it was going to be anything but straightforward. That is why I was so quick to flee to Tarshish. I know you are a gracious and compassionate God, slow to get angry and well, yes, full of love, a God who relents from sending calamity … but why for the city and not for me?

So just finish me off now. It's all been a waste of time and I'd rather die than live.

East of the City

Jonah son of Amittai crept away from the city, and the darkness that now surrounded him was all-engulfing. There was a track that led away from the door through which he'd just come – he could make out that much – and he followed it along, feeling increasingly despondent and fearful. It wasn't particularly cold, it wasn't particularly anything, just more dark and red and dusty than inside the city. It was an empty wilderness as far as he could tell; there were no buildings, or rubble where a building had once stood, no signs along the road of traffic or footfall. The quiet of the night and the glow of the city behind him were the only features he noticed. He would have had a lot of time to think if he wasn't so tired, but short of dropping down where he walked along the road, there seemed to be nowhere to lay his head. He decided to keep trudging forward until he did drop, till exhaustion overrode the lurking fear of being alone in this emptiness.

An hour or so had passed when up ahead he suddenly saw the outline of a shape – a small, slim building of some sort that seemed to have sprung up by the roadside. The outline grew stronger as he approached and there must have been a gentle light coming from inside the building, which revealed its shape and reality. Jonah picked up his feet and strode onwards with renewed purpose; if it was empty he could finally rest, if it wasn't … then, well, maybe whoever was there might be generous to an old prophet and let him squeeze in for a few hours.

On reaching it, he put his hand out and touched the rough wall of the low, narrow tower, and took a minute to catch his breath. He stopped and turned back to lean against the wall and watch the outline of the strangely still city behind him. A surge of anger rose up within him. He was exhausted, wiped out, spent and wasted, and for what? This was not what was supposed to happen.

The theory and, from his own experience, the working practice was that:

A) The prophet wandered about, warning of doom and destruction.
B) Nobody listened to him. He would be laughed at or things would be thrown at him or, worse, he would be thrown somewhere himself.
C) The aforementioned doom and destruction, in whatever form predicted, would happen. End of story.

So why in the name of all the planets had this not happened in the prescribed fashion? His reputation as a prophet (not that he had a great reputation, but he had one nonetheless) had bitten the dust. He looked at his feet and the bottom of his well-worn robes; dust was the operative word indeed.

'Jonah son of Amittai?'

The startled prophet spun round, nearly making a sorry end of his nose against the wall.

'What, me?' was all he could stammer in reply, as if there was any other lost, wandering soul in the shadows. How could somebody know who he was out here? How was it that everybody knew who he was all the time?

'Are you Jonah son of Amittai?' came the question once again. It was a checkpoint-bot who was speaking to him, not a person. There was some relief in that. Perhaps the city had communicated through that a mad old prophet was on the loose; nevertheless, Jonah thought it would be very unsatisfactory to shout and take his anger out on a bot.

Wearily Jonah answered, 'Well, yes, I am …'

'There is a message for you, Jonah son of Amittai.' The bot held out a screen with a post message ready to be read.

Had he come full circle, Jonah thought; was there never to be an end to this task?

'Can I rest here a while? Is there any room?' Jonah asked the bot in a futile attempt at ignoring the fact of the unread message. It was indeed futile:

'Jonah son of Amittai, you have a message,' repeated the bot.

Jonah bypassed the bot and went around the wall to find the entrance to the small checkpoint building. If he had to read the message (which he did, because the bot would not shut up if he didn't and he wouldn't know the first place to start when it came to dismantling or shutting down a bot), he at least wanted to know if there was room enough to lie down inside the building. He was angry but he was far more tired.

A long shelf, much like a desk, ran along one wall of the inside of the checkpoint hut. There were no blankets or cushions that he could see inside, which was logical, as the place was obviously never manned; he presumed that the bot represented the hub of communication out here. But it was the nearest thing to a bed that Jonah had seen this side of the city. He gathered the few odd pieces of equipment and papers that lay on the shelf, put them in a pile on the floor underneath and clambered up on to the shelf. He sat there for a minute while he decided in which direction to lie down – with his head towards the door or away from it. There was a dusky light above his head, which was pleasantly warming and unobtrusive.

The checkpoint-bot trundled into the building behind him and stopped in front of him and held the screen forward once more. Jonah smiled at the bot, his most winning smile, through gritted teeth and with a scowl that would in any other circumstance have a truly potent effect, but of course it made no dent whatsoever in the placid face of the bot. Before it could repeat itself, Jonah snatched the screen and with his thumbprint opened the message.

'Have you any right to be angry?'

That was the only line to be read and Jonah was in no doubt as to whom it was from. The desire to chuck the screen on the floor and stamp all over it until it was nothing but wires and cracked plastic was almost overwhelming. However, Jonah was not usually given to fierce emotional displays; it didn't often go hand in hand with propheting and there was also the fact that sometimes bots had been known to get possessive over their screens and such-like. He would not win that battle. So he resorted to a snarl at nobody in particular, and, with deliberate though restrained effort, he placed the screen on to the floor underneath him, then threw himself down flat on the shelf and turned over to face the wall. His faithful hat with the earflaps was the best pillow he could manage but it was little comfort under these very trying circumstances.

Footsteps of quite a large number were the first thing that he noticed on waking the next morning. It was morning, or at least some time in the day, because the light in the hut was off and there was a swathe of deep pink-orange sunlight hanging through the cloud and dusty fog, which he could see through the door and the small window opposite him. In the distance, Nineveh could also be seen through the window, a picture of stillness and calm framed especially for him.

He threw off the blanket that covered him and then stretched his feet down to reach the floor of the checkpoint hut and pottered towards the entrance. With his hands resting on the doorframe, he leant outside to see who or what was coming along the road.

An animal train coming from the city was heading up along the same road that he had taken towards the checkpoint, the bells around the beasts' necks clanging pastorally. The beasts themselves were quite clearly indigenous to the planet, with a range of horns along the spine, armour-plated flanks and heavy, dribbling jowls. Jonah recalled seeing the same variety tied up in front of the great gates of Nineveh in shackled herds, but he had never seen their like before then. They moved peacefully enough in a steady, resigned rhythm, driven from behind by herders dressed in little more than rags and dust.

The checkpoint-bot moved out towards them and counted the animals off as they passed, running a scanner over their ear tags and then scanning the passes on the wrists of the herders. Naturally the herders did not speak to the bot but when they saw Jonah they halted, unsure of his status or officialdom. On closer inspection they spied his prophet robes and turned to each other, whispering. Although they were merely animal keepers and drivers, they had some knowledge of what had recently occurred and enough wit to put two and two together and reach the correct conclusion.

Indicating their scant dress and the red dust on their skin, they fell down before Jonah and took handfuls of dust to pour over themselves once more, quietly wailing and murmuring words of repentance. One of their number suddenly stood, rubbing more handfuls of dust over the hides of the animals; the others got up from the ground and joined him, cooing carefully into the large ears of the beasts in their charge.

The bot went over to a stone mound, lifted a lid to reveal a tap and held out a bucket for the herders to fill with water to refresh both themselves and their animals. Normally eager to top up their water carriers, the herders stood back, shaking their heads and again bowing to the ground, starting up their murmured prayers again.

Jonah remembered the words of the king: 'Do not let them eat or drink … call urgently on God … so that we will not perish.'

Jonah closed his eyes on the scene and went back inside the hut; this was no longer anything to do with him. On the shelf where he had slept so soundly was a neatly folded blanket. A blanket: he had thrown it off just a few minutes earlier. But he had not gone to sleep with a blanket last night. Where had that come from? It must have been the bot. Perhaps it had covered him while he slept and then folded the covering neatly. As he was pondering this small miracle, the bot entered the hut, carrying a tray with a cup of water, some bread and some fruit.

'For Jonah son of Amittai.'

The tray was placed on the shelf next to the blanket, and the bot turned and went back outside to resume its duty and wait by the roadside.

'Well …' was all Jonah could manage. To say he was most grateful for the blanket and the water and the food was an understatement. Like a greedy schoolboy he sat on the shelf, legs swinging off the ground, watching the city through the window and eating this humble but most satisfactory breakfast; all thoughts of sorrowful, contrite animal herders were forgotten. He was not an ambitious or avaricious man; he did not demand a lot out of life; he had not chosen a lucrative career but he did appreciate his comforts, however mediocre. His job was done, his task completed. He would watch the city, at least for a while, to see how the destruction would play out, and then he would most absolutely and properly retire.

Nineveh lay still in its valley of red cloud and fog. All air traffic had ceased, all city traffic had halted; only the few necessary journeys on foot, like the animal herders', continued with demure restraint. The king walked among his people, along the streets, observing the signs of dereliction and violence that had marked the city. Ganglords and corrupt dignitaries, slave traffickers and flesh marketers all gathered as he passed by, falling with pain-filled cries of despair at the consequences of their evil ways. For some unforeseen reason, the timing had been so right; the people knew they had been so wrong, and now those who had so perfunctorily dealt out destruction and death to others now faced their own. The words that Jonah had spoken, the words that as a prophet he had been commissioned to speak, had cracked home, slicing flesh from bone and bone from marrow. Never had a city been plagued by its own evil torture in such a way, and never had a city heard the call to turn around and responded in such a way.

The checkpoint-bot served Jonah all day long. From who knew where, it produced meals and water, even a cup of tea and a slice of cake in the afternoon. Jonah sat outside the checkpoint in the best of the weather, stretched out on a low reclining chair, watching the very little activity that was going on; it felt like the first real rest he had had in a long, long time. By the evening, the view of Nineveh had not changed, but Jonah thought that in these circumstances he could wait a while longer to see how it would happen. He had decided not to be angry today.

The prophecy had talked about 'forty more days' before any destruction might occur, but Jonah assumed that this was just a figure of speech; with a place as bad as this, there was no hope. The best the people could do was to leave. It was strange, he thought after a while, that there were not droves of folk pouring out of the gates with all their worldly goods in tow. He waggled his toes in the breeze and thanked the bot for the top-up of tea that had just been poured.

That night he curled up once more on the shelf, with the blanket and a proper pillow for his head, and drifted off to sleep, wondering whether the mass exodus from the city might begin tomorrow.

His straggly beard was stiff with icicles by the next morning; a sudden cold snap had blown up from the far side of the planet, as it often did at that time of the year – a fact of which Jonah was quite unaware. He shivered and reached out to pull the blanket up to his chin, but it wasn't there. It had not just slipped down on to the floor in the night; it had utterly disappeared. His fingers were blue with cold, his feet begging for warm woolly socks.

'Hey!' he called, hoping the bot would come back from outside and shut the door behind it and bring some of that delicious, hot, steaming tea.

No bot appeared, and then a tremendous blast of wind shook the checkpoint, slamming the old door on its hinges until it broke off, smashing into pieces against the wall.

Jonah scrambled off the bench and poked his head outside. He could see the bot in the middle of the road, immobile and half buried in frozen red dust. If he attempted to call out to the bot, his words were just ripped away, up into the whirling fury of wind. Struggling against the elements, Jonah left the relative shelter of the hut and went out towards the place where it stood. Up close now, he reached out and stabbed at the bot. 'Hey, you!'

With a creak the bot toppled over, the direction and force of the wind finally winning. The bot was silent and lifeless, unflickering and unresponsive. Jonah bent down in the dust and fingered the controls on its torso; he noticed that several wires had come loose and the lights that ran along its front plate were blown out. Ice had got inside its visor and had cracked right through the place where it might have had eyes.

He himself was now frozen to the bone and his mouth, ears and eyes were full of dust; he could hardly feel his fingers or toes. The only place of safety was the meagre shelter of the checkpoint hut.

Where was the sense in all of this? That's what Jonah wanted to know. What had happened to his poor bot? It had served him well and faithfully, far better than anything he could have imagined, and he had dreamt last night of taking it home with him to comfort and care for him in his long-awaited retirement. He had begun to make plans, and so suddenly it had all been swept away from him.

'I just want to die!' In his dry, cold and cracked voice, Jonah cried out, knowing full well that there was no one around to hear.

The screen that the bot had, only yesterday, given him with a message to read bleeped. It shone in the darkness under the shelf, where it had been left, all but forgotten.

Someone had heard his cry and someone had something to say to Jonah …

One Hundred and Twenty Thousand People

Tucked up in a moderate-sized cabin (but still with a decent view) on a top-of-the-range, luxury cruise liner, a lone prophet sat thinking on the events of the past. It had been a long time since he was called by God to go on an adventure, and he wondered, even though he was now fully retired, if it would ever occur again.

'A prosperous city of well over one hundred and twenty thousand people, which in recent years has flourished and proved the critics wrong, countering its previously damning reputation, Nineveh lies at the far edge of our system. With its various moons and commanding landscape, its magnificent architecture and ancient libraries, the city and planet of the same name now offer the perfect holiday destination. In Nineveh there is most definitely something for everyone.'

Jonah son of Amittai switched off his earpiece; he didn't really want to listen to any more. Instead he watched the rich blackness of space out of the viewing window that made up one side of his cabin. He had promised himself a cruise, a proper holiday, all planned and paid for – no cheap last-minute deals this time. It was scheduled to last four years and two months, visiting all the major local planets in their system and guaranteed not to involve any accidental comets or any such other disasters. He glanced down at the muddle of wiring that lay in his lap, and sighed.

'Well, I should have agreed to cheat and buy a ready-made model. I'm an old prophet, not a Jim.'

As part of his true retirement he had decided to take up, with little success so far, a new hobby: he wanted to make his own bot, just like the one from Nineveh. He had brought the Build-Your-Own-Bot-Kit on the cruise with him, hoping that at the end of four years and two months he might have something to show for it. So far he had opened the box, studied the contents and the instruction manual, written in a myriad different languages, and attempted to untangle the bundle of wiring.

The cruiser would be stopping off in Nineveh in several hours' time, halting first to sample the delights of the now system-famous deluxe restaurant on Mari's landing station. Jonah knew he would step out to eat there, if only to see if the old 'rules and regulations' notices were still plastered over the ceiling, but he would not be setting foot on Nineveh itself.

A message appeared on his new personal mobile screen, which could be folded up and carried around or clipped on to one's chair or by one's bedside, or almost anywhere really. The message read: 'Please note, we will be docking on the moon station of Mari in one hour. Please remember to bring all identification passes and credit facilities with you. Thank you.'

Although he was quite used to these informative, helpful and very rarely annoying messages popping up on his screen, they always made him jump. They always took him back to that scant, cold checkpoint hut outside the walls of Nineveh. They always took him back to his conversation with God …

No cold weather had ever been as cold as it had been that morning, that whole long day in the wastelands of Nineveh. Without the city walls, without the buildings and gates to protect him, he had never felt so vulnerable. It was a surprising thing to say when he had truly been through so many terrifying situations, leading up to that event, which could quite accurately be described as vulnerable-making.

The screen that Jonah had found on the floor of the hut that morning had flickered into life and, in answer to Jonah's irrelevant cry that he might no longer live but just be allowed to die, God had answered.

'Do you have a right to be angry about the bot?'

That had been the message and Jonah had not liked it. Of course he had a right to be angry. It had been a very useful bot, never a bot like it, and yet a mere change in the weather had spelled disaster. Why wasn't he allowed to stay there with the bot to look after him? That hadn't been asking too much, surely?

Jonah remembered his reply. 'I do!' he had yelled. 'I am angry enough to die!'

God, ever gentle, ever compassionate, ever wise, had spoken: 'Oh Jonah, you have been so concerned about this bot, though you didn't design it or construct it. You just found it. It suddenly sprang up here, ready to greet you and give you your message, and then overnight it suddenly died ...'

Jonah had known all of that but it hadn't made things any easier to deal with or understand. It had been a moment of personal crisis, and how could he have known that God would not forget him?

The conversation had continued as God spoke again: 'But Nineveh has more than a hundred and twenty thousand people who cannot tell their right hand from their left, and many animals too ...'

'Yes, I know all that!' Jonah's anger had not diminished. 'But you asked me to go and tell them you were going to destroy them all. The city is evil, beyond all hope.'

The last message on the screen had revealed the heart of God: there is no one, ever, beyond all hope. In that little ramshackle hut, in that dry cold wilderness, Jonah had lost all hope; he was only a prophet, only a man who had limited wisdom, imagination and grace. God is limitless: that had been the message.

'Should I not be concerned about that great city?'

Jonah had had no answer, nothing to say. He had known that destruction would not now fall on Nineveh, at least not in the next forty days and then probably not for a long time after. If the king and the people proved to be as truly repentant as they appeared to be, then he knew God, and he knew the tremendous heart that would respond in love and mercy.

There had been nothing left for him there, back in that checkpoint building. He had looked out at the city one last time and had then set off along the road, following the footsteps of the herders – well, at least, in their presumed footsteps, because the weather had changed the road into a smooth untouched path of tiny, sugar-like, dust-ice granules. It had been a tough journey to take with the wind still cutting across his frail body; even his hat had struggled to remain in place and fulfil its duty. He had been counting on the slim chance that the herders had been aiming for somewhere in particular; at least he had had comparative daylight with which to make some headway.

About three hours later, he'd felt the urge to fall by the wayside and metamorphose himself into a collapsed and useless pile of prophet, where people might pass in future days and point to an indistinguishable mound and say, 'Ah, there was the prophet, the one they called Jonah son of Amittai. It was he who called for the destruction of Nineveh!'

When that thought had almost been too much, Jonah had spied some shapes and shadows that looked like a collection of buildings, a village of sorts. Just as he had hurried to the hut before, he had stepped forward once more, with fresh vigour, in the hope of shelter and a way to escape this disappointing planet.

Warmth and even warmer food can do a lot to lift a prophet's despondency, and so it had been that Jonah found eventual comfort in the form of a woodshed and some kind-hearted, though slightly suspicious people. They had heard from the herders about the goings-on in the city and about a prophet who had turned everything upside down, even to the drawing out of the king who never left his perfect chambers. The normally busy sky, filled with traffic and lights and noises, had been weirdly silent for several days; the people hoped that they could feed the prophet and pack him up with provisions and send him quickly on his way, in case he might prophesy against them too. So they had smiled and given him everything they thought he might need, laying it before him and backing slowly out of the woodshed, which, it had been decided, was the least dangerous place to put a prophet.

Jonah had not cared at all; he had never been one for company. That's why being a prophet had suited him so well from the beginning. He had spent a couple of days sleeping in the straw, trying to block out his conversation with God, trying to forget everything that had happened since leaving his own little home in what had seemed to him like an age and a half.

Breaking free of his thoughts, Jonah could tell that they were about to land and dock into the station on Mari; one got used to the familiar noises that were part and parcel of cruiser manoeuvres. He carefully placed the muddle of wires back into the box and, after several attempts and a few creaks and groans, got himself up from the lounger where he had been watching space go by. After a brief visit to the utility area to wash and brush up and change into some smarter robes, he was ready for lunch.

There would be a queue; it would therefore, in his opinion, be easier and pleasanter to wait a while, while the more eager, pushy lot elbowed to the front. Jonah stood by the rails outside his cabin along the viewing pathway that circled the cruiser, watching the great expanse of space. Right below him was the giant planet of Nineveh hanging in space and promising a very good holiday to all. The red cloudy shell that had previously encased the planet had greatly diminished, he noticed. Jonah had heard that their manufacturing plants had had a clean-up and that money was now being poured into strengthening their industries rather than squeezing out every drop of blood, no matter the cost. Even though he couldn't actually see the city itself, Jonah knew it was there under the thick atmosphere and he shuddered at the powerful cocktail of feelings that came flooding back.

The villagers had been so very relieved when he had finally decided to move on. Their profusion of kindness had almost made him feel like changing his mind and staying: they had been nearly as good to him as the bot. But thankfully for everyone concerned, he had said his vaguely fond but most appropriate farewells and left for the next outpost, which had amounted to another day's journey on foot. There, the villagers had sincerely assured him, he would find someone prepared to fly him away from their planet. 'Away away!' they had gestured with much smiling and much hoping.

Fitted for the road, he had strode out along the track and had been glad to note that the ferocious weather of the previous few days had all but ceased and that the slight scarlet hue of settled dust was enough to brighten his way.

Most out-in-the-sticks places seem to have an 'Old Jim' character lurking and tinkering in a machine shop on the edges of civilisation, and Jonah had found the next outpost no exception. The man was maybe a bit younger than the Jim he had found on Kittim; however, this character was singular – there was only one of him. That was no disadvantage, though, and with only two hands he had still been a force of invention, construction and repair, with a knowledge that seemed to have been imbibed just by looking at anything with a cog, screw or widget.

The man had asked no questions; he had not appeared to even notice Jonah's robes and thereby make the obvious deduction. He had merely seen an old man who wanted a swift exit out of there – someone new to educate in the ways of cogs and screws and widgets, who was willing to pay for the privilege.

Jonah had crammed himself into the compact transporter, readying himself to keep his eyes and ears shut. As the craft had lurched off the ground, a great weight had fallen from his heart, or wherever it was that had felt so heavy, and he had happily realised that he was just a prophet journeying home once more.

'Should I not be concerned about that great city?'

'What's that?' queried a voice behind him. Jonah was not aware that he had spoken out loud. A young couple standing behind him in the queue were now looking him up and down.

'Ah well ...' he fumbled with his words. 'I mean, what I mean to say is that that is a great city, down there.' He pointed downwards to the planet, where he hoped the city of Nineveh lay.

'Been there before, have you?' asked the young woman, her three large eyes, each a different colour, watching his face.

'Well ...' Jonah coughed and wondered what he could say, very politely of course, to make them go away. 'In actual fact, I ...'

He needn't have worried: he was saved (as once before) by a loudspeaker.

'For all our passengers cruising with us, please have your identification papers at the ready. Welcome to Mari. The restaurant has been exclusively reserved for our passengers. Please take your time to enjoy the local delicacies before, later on, we make our way down into Nineveh. The restaurant has been refurbished in recent times but still retains some of its earlier vintage features, notably the unique ceiling décor, which reveals a more colourful and troubled past where the rule of law did not reach. Thank you and enjoy your visit.'

The meal was excellent, although most folk managed to come away with cricked necks (due to too much ceiling gazing) and were therefore not so sure it had been worth it. The more intelligent had saved their necks and had instead purchased a book of postcards, each one a small reproduction of the original floating ceiling posters.

Jonah thought he might do the same and send a few to his neighbours back home, to the person minding his vegetables and his roof tiles and the other person borrowing and hopefully maintaining his scooterer until he returned. Thinking about it, though, sending someone a postcard telling them not to spit in the aisles or the food, or not to pinch the waitresses in places they wouldn't want to be pinched might be misconstrued. It was enough to have been there under more pleasant circumstances, to have enjoyed his meal as requested by the loudspeaker, and to have left it at that.

It suddenly struck him that he would never be the same again. All propheting and the oddness that that already implied aside, he had been part of something far beyond himself. God, the God of the planets, of the magnificence of unending space, of the incomprehensible grand design of world after world – the God of all that and more had asked him, Jonah, the reluctant, feeble, elderly and occasionally pompous prophet, to do a job.

It had seemed so awful at the time (and, relatively speaking, it had been rather awful), so much bigger than anything he had previously been asked to do, and yet, at the same time, so pointless and a waste of resources. He had worried and complained and fussed about the outcome and his own poor situation, and yet at every turn he had been provided for and trusted to do his job faithfully. The heart of God was for ever big; all the great depths of space surrounding them were a drop in the bucket compared to that heart, and that same heart was unfathomably bothered about him and bothered about everyone. He wished he had had the imagination to grasp it all. Shutting his eyes on the vastness of all that was visible, just for a moment, he remembered the words of God …

'Nineveh has more than one hundred and twenty thousand people who cannot tell their right hand from their left. Should I not be concerned about them?'

THE BOOK OF JONAH

Jonah Disobeys the LORD

1 One day the LORD spoke to Jonah son of Amittai.
He said, "Go to Nineveh, that great city, and speak out against it; I am aware how wicked its people are."

Jonah, however, set out in the opposite direction in order to get away from the LORD. He went to Joppa, where he found a ship about to go to Spain. He paid his fare and went aboard with the crew to sail to Spain, where he would be away from the LORD.

But the LORD sent a strong wind on the sea, and the storm was so violent that the ship was in danger of breaking up.

The sailors were terrified and cried out for help, each one to his own god. Then, in order to lessen the danger, they threw the cargo overboard. Meanwhile, Jonah had gone below and was lying in the ship's hold, sound asleep.

The captain found him there and said to him, "What are you doing asleep? Get up and pray to your god for help. Maybe he will feel sorry for us and spare our lives."

The sailors said to one another, "Let's draw lots and find out who is to blame for getting us into this danger." They did so, and Jonah's name was drawn.

So they said to him: "Now then, tell us! Who is to blame for this? What are you doing here? What country do you come from? What is your nationality?"

"I am a Hebrew," Jonah answered. "I worship the LORD, the God of heaven, who made land and sea."

Jonah went on to tell them that he was running away from the LORD.

The sailors were terrified, and said to him, "That was an awful thing to do!"

The storm was getting worse all the time, so the sailors asked him, "What should we do to you to stop the storm?"

Jonah answered, "Throw me into the sea, and it will calm down. I know it is my fault that you are caught in this violent storm."

Instead, the sailors tried to get the ship to shore, rowing with all their might. But the storm was getting worse and worse, and they got nowhere.

So they cried out to the LORD, "O LORD, we pray, don't punish us with death for taking this man's life! You, O LORD, are responsible for all this; it is your doing."

Then they picked Jonah up and threw him into the sea, and it calmed down at once.

This made the sailors so afraid of the LORD that they offered a sacrifice and promised to serve him.

At the LORD's command a large fish swallowed Jonah, and he was inside the fish for three days and nights.

Jonah's Prayer

2 From deep inside the fish Jonah prayed to the LORD his God:

"In my distress, O LORD, I called to you,
    and you answered me.
From deep in the world of the dead
    I cried for help, and you heard me.

You threw me down into the depths,
    to the very bottom of the sea,
    where the waters were all round me,
    and all your mighty waves rolled over me.

I thought I had been banished from your presence
    and would never see your holy Temple again.

The water came over me and choked me;
the sea covered me completely,
and seaweed was wrapped round my head.

I went down to the very roots of the mountains,
into the land whose gates lock shut for ever.
But you, O LORD my God,
brought me back from the depths alive.

When I felt my life slipping away,
then, O LORD, I prayed to you,
and in your holy Temple you heard me.

Those who worship worthless idols
have abandoned their loyalty to you.

But I will sing praises to you;
I will offer you a sacrifice
and do what I have promised.
Salvation comes from the LORD!"

Then the LORD ordered the fish to spew Jonah up on the beach, and it did.

Jonah Obeys the LORD

3 Once again the LORD spoke to Jonah.
He said, "Go to Nineveh, that great city, and proclaim to the people the message I have given you."

So Jonah obeyed the LORD and went to Nineveh, a city so large that it took three days to walk through it.

Jonah started through the city, and after walking a whole day, he proclaimed, "In forty days Nineveh will be destroyed!"

The people of Nineveh believed God's message. So they decided that everyone should fast, and all the people, from the greatest to the least, put on sackcloth to show that they had repented.

When the king of Nineveh heard about it, he got up from his throne, took off his robe, put on sackcloth, and sat down in ashes.

He sent out a proclamation to the people of Nineveh: "This is an order from the king and his officials: no one is to eat anything; all persons, cattle, and sheep are forbidden to eat or drink.

All persons and animals must wear sackcloth. Everyone must pray earnestly to God and must give up his wicked behaviour and his evil actions.

Perhaps God will change his mind; perhaps he will stop being angry, and we will not die!"

God saw what they did; he saw that they had given up their wicked behaviour. So he changed his mind and did not punish them as he had said he would.

Jonah's Anger and God's Mercy

4 Jonah was very unhappy about this and became angry.

So he prayed, "LORD, didn't I say before I left home that this is just what you would do? That's why I did my best to run away to Spain! I knew that you are a loving and merciful God, always patient, always kind, and always ready to change your mind and not punish.

Now, LORD, let me die. I am better off dead than alive."

The LORD answered, "What right have you to be angry?"

Jonah went out east of the city and sat down. He made a shelter for himself and sat in its shade, waiting to see what would happen to Nineveh.

Then the LORD God made a plant grow up over Jonah to give him some shade, so that he would be more comfortable. Jonah was extremely pleased with the plant.

But at dawn the next day, at God's command, a worm attacked the plant, and it died.

After the sun had risen, God sent a hot east wind, and Jonah was about to faint from the heat of the sun beating down on his head. So he wished he were dead. "I am better off dead than alive," he said.

But God said to him, "What right have you to be angry about the plant?"

Jonah replied, "I have every right to be angry — angry enough to die!"

The LORD said to him, "This plant grew up in one night and disappeared the next; you didn't do anything for it, and you didn't make it grow — yet you feel sorry for it!

How much more, then, should I have pity on Nineveh, that great city. After all, it has more than 120,000 innocent children in it, as well as many animals!"

About the author

Jo Sheringham has been writing, on and off, for many years. Three novels, already available online, have themes of mystery and futuristic fantasy and include a retelling of the Old Testament story of Daniel.

As a great believer in 'less is more' (not necessarily an excuse to write two words instead of 200) she is interested in the small, invisible and ordinary events in life, which often prove to have far greater and more meaningful consequences than we at first imagine.

With four grown-up daughters, Jo lives in Wiltshire with her husband and is part of a vibrant, active church family.